SINGING DAGGER

BLADES OF VENGEANCE

ROWAN THALIA

JENÉE ROBINSON

Rebekah,
Always be yourself,
unless you can be a
mermaid. Then be
a mermaid! ♡ —Jenée Robinson

Peace, love and dicks,

Rowan Thalia

Copyright Notice

Copyright © 2022 Rowan Thalia & Jenée Robinson
Cover Art by: EVE's Graphic Design LLC
Editing by: Michelle's Edits

All rights reserved. No part of this publication may be reproduced, distributed, or transmitted in any form or by any means, including photocopying, recording, or other electronic or mechanical methods, without the publisher's prior written permission, except with brief quotations in book reviews.

Any references to historical events, real people, or real places are used fictitiously. Names, characters, and places are products of the authors' imagination.

❦ Created with Vellum

ARI

My eyes open, but my mind is foggy. The details of the room start to fill in, disorienting me for a moment. Where's the water? My body won't move. It feels so heavy. A cool breeze tickles the side of my face, and I turn my head. Iron bars cover the open window, a view of the night sky bringing me back to reality.

"I no longer swim in the ocean, but this isn't the palace, either. Am I still dreaming?" I whisper. The paralysis lifts, and I sit up. One circular stone wall surrounds me, except for the iron bars that cover the doorway on the opposite side of the room. Chills run down my spine at the dank interior. The cell is empty save the small bed and a metal fountain for relieving oneself. Another wave of anxiety washes over me. How did I get here? Where's my husband?

"Eric?" I wheeze, shivering. The light blanket covering me is of no real comfort. Looking down, I notice I'm still wearing the blue dress I wore this morning. Well, what I think was this morning, anyway.

I remember looking into the mirror, twirling to be sure my shells didn't create a weird profile. You'd be surprised at what odd items humans wear underneath their clothing.

Pushing the scratchy blanket aside, my feet hit the cold floor, and I wobble, still not fully awake. My mind is a fog of colors and scenes that I can't quite comprehend. Using the metal bed frame, I steady myself to stand. The only sound greeting me is the screaming of the wind rushing through the room. Almost losing balance, I grab the floor before my face hits the rough surface. Before getting up, I gasp at the sight of dark stains along the hem of my skirt.

My throat tightens; I need to find out where I am. "Hello?" Though my voice goes nowhere in this cold, dark space, I manage to call out.

Reality hits me like the weight of a ton of clams. Something is very wrong. Am I being held captive? But why? Rubbing my face, I force my memory back to no avail. My brain is a cloud of murk. Getting my land legs back, I surge toward the door on my hands and knees. Holding tight to the rails, I peer down the long corridor. A faint light flickers from around the corner. Heart in my throat, I listen for any clue as to where I am. Humans put terrible people in; what's the word? Jail. I'm in prison. But why?

A tightness grips my chest as snippets from the day flood my memory. I remember being on a boat with Eric, Max lolling his tongue as he watched the fish. The sun was bright, and my father and sisters came to the surface to visit. I smile faintly, remembering their faces. After that, we had dinner at the palace with Eric's parents. We ended the evening with a carriage ride home to our small tower behind the castle. Then, blackness. A scream. Blood. Hands gripping my arms.

"Eric!" I scream as loud as my voice will carry. This must be some trick.

"You're awake!" The deep male voice precedes the very round figure speaking. He steps closer to the bars, blocking the faint light.

Frightened, I crab-walk backward. This can't be right. "Who are you? Where am I? Where's Eric?" My voice cracks. Fresh, salty air rushes through the window, and I take it in deeply as the walls seem to close in on me.

"You're a jittery, little thing, aren't ya? I'm Jax, the jailer of Tirulia. Eric is lying in a bloody heap where you left him, or don't you remember that? Are you ready to confess to your crime? The King wants to know why you would do such a thing before he sentences you to death," The man jingles a set of keys in his hands.

"Confess? I've done no such thing. I would never!" I clutch the locket Eric bought for our first anniversary.

The man laughs, holding his ample belly. He shakes his head and walks away, leaving his faint aroma of grease behind. My stomach turns at the smell. There must have been a mistake; I don't belong here.

Pacing the small cell, I frantically try to piece together the events that led to my imprisonment. Tears fill my eyes, and my stomach turns acidic. My mind draws a blank, and my breath catches in my throat. Then a blurry image comes to focus of Eric slumped on the sofa, his face blue, blood dripping from his hand onto the floor. My screams filled the sitting room as guards swarmed and drug me away. If I could turn off the vision, I would. It's too terrible to see.

Trying to clear the ugliness from my sight, I bring up an image of my wedding day. I squeeze my eyes as if closing them will block out the gory scene of my broken memory. "Father, help me," a tear runs down my cheek; it's no use. Triton doesn't bother with life on land. Besides, his answer would be to wipe out the entire town with a tsunami, and that's not the answer.

A squawk calls my attention. Two white feathers float down to the stone floor from the window. I look up, and a sliver of hope warms me as Scuttle appears behind the bars. Any familiar face is a boon at the moment. "Heyya kid, I heard you were in trouble with the humans," my feathered friend says, craning his neck from side to side. "The beach is all abuzz with blabber. Tell me, how'd you get mixed up in this commotion?"

"I can't remember." I sob. "Oh, Scuttle, what am I going to do?"

"Should I ask your father? Sebastian and Flounder? You tell me where to fly, and I'll go." Scuttle paces the small ledge.

"No!" I put my hands up. "Definitely not my father. Who knows what he would do if he found out I was in here." I point to the bars. "Go find Sebastian and Flounder. Keep my location under wraps otherwise." I shoo him off his perch.

Flying half-crooked, Scuttle salutes. "You got it, kid." I watch him fly away, a sinking feeling in my chest.

Somehow, I've got to get out of here and find out what happened. There aren't any humans I trust besides Eric, and—if the jailor is to be believed—he may be gone. Hysteria threatens to creep in as images of a blood-soaked room bombard me. Gasping for breath, I kneel by the bed. My head rests against the hard mattress, and I grip the threadbare, gray blanket as I allow my mind to recreate the missing moments. Nothing in my memory points to me being a murderer.

I'm sure I did not hurt my husband, and whoever did will pay. Resolve sinks in my bones, and I stand. Peering out into the night sky, I focus all my will on one thought. Besides my father, only one deity could help me now. Please, Moryana, hear my plea. Let vengeance be mine. However, it may come.

I move back into the shadows of my new home as if that will help me disappear from this nightmare. A shiver runs through me while I ponder what the humans plan to do with me. They will give me a trial, but will that be fair? I was a mermaid most of my life. Our punishments in the ocean are different than they are here.

How will I defend myself? The only money at my disposal is Eric's. Will they deny me that as well? Being in this unfortunate state makes me miss my fins, friends, and the freedom of the ocean. I rise and decide I need to find a way out of here. Running fingers over every inch of the walls, I seek any weakness. But no such luck.

The jailer returns. The only way I know is because he hits the metal on the other side of the door, bringing me back to my sad reality. With a sigh, I still my fingers from their endless searching of the slick walls.

"Confess," he whispers. Just the sound of his voice has my skin crawling.

"I have nothing to confess," answering him for what feels like the hundredth time, I turn away from the sight of his greasy fingers. He must be too thick to get it through his skull.

"No matter, the townspeople are readying their pitchforks," he chuckles as he rattles his keys. I press back into the shadows, ignoring his taunts, remembering my last birthday in the sea.

Flounder and I went for a swim. I finally talked my best friend into searching the shipwrecks for human treasures.

"Why did you want to come out here again, Ariel?"

"Thingamabobs, Flounder. Just imagine what we can find here. I can't wait to collect some things for Scuttle to tell us about."

"But what about the sharks that swim this part of the ocean?"

"We will make it quick, and they will never know we were here. You can look out for me if you're worried about it."

"No, I think I'll stay with you."

I smiled because I knew he wouldn't get too far from me. There was so much to look at, but I chose a few crates; that's where they hide the best things. I was filling my bag when Flounder and I were no longer alone.

"S-s-s-s-shark!" Flounder stutters..

Of course, there was a shark here. The vast beasts tended to hang out around the shipwrecks because humans tried to recover what had sunk. Who wouldn't want a little snack?

"Don't be a guppy, Flounder." I scolded until I turned; sure enough, white, pointed teeth were headed straight for us!

"You better move those flippers, Flounder. That shark looks like he is ready for a snack."

"Ari!" Flounder whined.

"Fine, get in the bag. You better hurry. I'm not waiting all day."

It was the fastest he ever swam. Soon, he was snuggling into the depths of my bag. We made our escape and went to Scuttle with my finds.

What I wouldn't give to have those carefree swims now.

At long last, the ragged breathing of my jailer quiets down. Without the distraction, I could get some rest. I'm afraid of what dream may come, but sleep will help pass the time until my friends can plan my rescue.

The old cot creaks a little as I climb atop it. It's not that I weigh a lot. The springs have never been oiled. Tucking an arm under my head, I try my best not to think of what the stain on the mattress is from and curl myself into a ball.

"Oh, Eric, I vow that I will make this right. I'm so

sorry that this happened, my love," I whisper into the shadows as if he could hear my words.

I hum the lullaby my father would sing me when I swam to his chambers after a nightmare. The melody was one thing that could soothe my nerves just enough that I was able to sleep.

ARI

With Scuttle gone, there's nothing to keep me company besides the occasional grunt or cough from the jailer. Laying on the hard cot, I attempt to rest, but my mind will not abide by my wishes. Head spinning, I toss and turn on the small mattress.

Minutes seem like hours as I stare at the stone ceiling. A spider is weaving its web in the corner, which delights me insofar that something living is in the cell with me. Mesmerized, I track its movements as it creates a large hexagon that fills a gap left where part of the stone broke off. How long do spiders live? Caught up in the tiny creature, I pass the time until a familiar clicking catches my attention.

Turning my gaze to the floor, I watch a small crab squeeze through the bars of my cell. My spirits rise, and I sit up to greet my old friend and mentor. Before I can set foot on the floor, a red fog begins to rise from the ground. Soon the room is filled. Confused, I try to wave the smoke away.

"Sebastian?" I cough.

The small crustacean begins to shake, clicking on the floor erratically. Breath catching in my throat, I scoot to the corner of the bed. The smoke thickens until it's impossible to see anything. Not knowing what else to do, I creep forward until my hands are at the edge of the bed.

I stare at where I think the crab was located before the room was filled with the cloud. Instead of my friend, a curvy woman dressed in sheer, red fabric appears, and my jaw drops open. Cheeks flaming, I take in her wide hips and perky breasts without meaning to do so. Gold clasps hold the light fabric at each shoulder, allowing it to billow and cascade around her. A flash of metal in her hand draws my attention. She's holding a shiny dagger with a giant ruby on the handle. I look up to see her piercing, purple eyes settle on me and her ruby lips widen into a smile.

"If I'm not mistaken, you require my assistance, child. Allow me to introduce myself. I am the Goddess of vengeance and death. I have many names and forms, but you may call me Moryana." She tilts her head to the side as if assessing my worth.

"I, uhh," my tongue seems caught in my mouth as I fumble to respond. "Yes, Goddess, I find myself in great need." I bow as low as the bed will allow.

Moryana lifts me by the chin. "The winds whisper of your peril, but they do not tell all. Death at the hand of humans will not do for a daughter of Triton; she clicks her tongue. "Tell me, child, why are you in this predicament? Shouldn't you be in Atlantica? Whatever did you do to your fin?"

Unsure where to start, I clear my throat. Moryana drops my chin and settles beside me, waiting. Wringing my hands, I try to find my voice. The room seems hotter than before, and I almost panic. The last time I spoke to anyone besides my father about my troubles, I created a whole world of problems for myself. Determined not to mess up again, I pull myself together.

"I gave up my life in Atlantica to marry my true love, Eric, who is ... was a prince in this land. Something happened last night, and I'm being accused of his death," I straighten my shoulders, looking the Goddess in the eye. "I committed no such act."

"Easy enough to solve. I can help you, but as with anything dealing with a deity—my help comes at a price." She turns the ornate dagger in her hand. The symmetry of her statement against my last deal with the sea witch isn't lost on me, but I've nowhere else to turn.

"Whatever it is, I will pay it," I vow, hoping I don't regret it.

"Very well," Moryana stands, tapping the end of the knife in one hand. "This dagger will aid you in finding those responsible for harming you and yours in any way. The job will not be easy, and you will not be able to do so alone. The dagger will tell you when you've found a trusted ally by glowing. Only when you've assembled what it deems worthy will you be able to fully activate its magic. In payment, you'll also be in charge of avenging my bloodline. The dagger shall lead you when the time comes. To activate the dagger, you must use that which is of the most value in you." She chuckles, and for a moment, the sea witch's face flashes before my eyes.

"You mean my voice?" I gulp, remembering how it was taken from me.

"Just so. When you hum, lay the dagger in your palm like so." Moryana opens her hand, and I let out a breath, glad that my voice will still be my own. "The dagger will point in the direction you must travel, but it will only work when you are within range of those you seek. You will have to work to find your marks. The closer you come, the more the ruby will glow. Do you understand?" I nod, staring at the oval gemstone. "Since you are a daughter of Triton, it will also allow you to shift into a form more accustomed to swimming. Heed this warning, you will be changed once you touch this dagger. Everything you once knew about yourself will be overshadowed by the blade's will, rendering you nearly unrecognizable to those you once knew. The heat of vengeance will overcome you, and you will think of nothing else until all enemies are vanquished." She gestures to me. "Rise, Ari, wielder of the Singing Dagger, and accept your fate. "

A lump forms in my throat as I stand and offer my hand. Moryana places the dagger in my palm. The hilt warms as I close my fingers around it, and a hushed whisper emits from the weapon, "*Vengeance*."

Warmth radiates from the hilt up my arm. I wince, and the heat rushes throughout my body, exploding at my core. A sudden shift clicks in my mind, then I find myself thirsting for the death of my enemies. Moryana wasn't kidding. Looking down at the weapon, I smirk.

SINGING DAGGER

The dagger vibrates as if in acknowledgment before it begins to cool. Closing my eyes, I begin to hum a familiar melody.

When I open my eyes, I'm no longer in the cell. The thunder of waves surrounds me, and cool water splashes at my face. Circling slowly, I recognize the space as my secret cave a mile away from the castle. I've spent many long hours here visiting Flounder. My first thought is to call my friend. Instead, I rush to one of the many trunks I have stashed in the corner—some habits die hard, I suppose. There must be something I can use to keep the Singing Dagger close to my side.

I continue digging till I find what human women carry their goods in. A purse, I was told it is called. My knowledge of some human things still needs to be improved. This will be an excellent place for the dagger when it isn't used, and I can carry it easily. Satisfied with my find, I pull the strap over my shoulder and place the weapon within. So intent on my mission, I almost missed the splashing behind me.

"It's about time you got here, Flounder," I say as I turn to face my friend.

"How did you escape?" The blue and yellow fish pokes his head out of the water.

"It's nice to see you, too, Flounder," I admonish.

"Are the rumors true? Eric is dead?"

"I don't know," I answer. I sit just at the edge of the water but don't have the guts to touch it yet. The Goddess's words ring in my ears that I can shift forms, that I am part of both worlds once more.

"What's on your face?"

Shrugging, I scoop a handful of water and splash it on my face, assuming I have grime or dirt from being held in that filthy cell. "Did I get it?"

"No, it's not dirt but some decoration on your face. Did you let someone write on your temples?"

"What? No!" I peek into the water, trying to get a good look at my reflection. I have to hold in a gasp when I notice what Flounder was asking about. Moryana told me the blade would transform me, but I didn't think too heavily of her statement. These tattoos on my forehead and temples are the first place to change so far. There is no way to tell if they are the last.

Do I confide in my little, fishy friend? That I took a dagger and chose vengeance over human justice?

"Where is Sebastian? I figured he'd love to be here and lecture me about humans."

"I'm here," my crabby friend pipes in. He's a little more stealthy in the water than Flounder.

"There is no 'I told you so' this time. If the rumors are true, you not only lost the love of your life but your freedom. Tell me what happened, Ariel." I flinch at my old name, which brings a tinge of pain to my temples.

"First, call me Ari from here out." I stare him down so that he knows I'm serious. "Everything seems so far away; I'm not sure what happened. This evening, I woke up in a cell. I was confused, and then a man came to me and told me to confess to murdering Eric," I frown. "My memory of the time before is foggy. I only have a few flashes of Eric, which are forever seared in my brain," I say, almost absently. It's funny how differently bringing up the memory feels now that I have the dagger.

Focusing back on Sebastian, I continue, "I'm not sure if Eric was dead, but his face was blue, and blood dripped from his hand." I stared into the water. *What I wouldn't give to pinch myself and wake from this nightmare.*

"Ari, that doesn't explain how you were in jail or got out." Sebastian clicks his claw at me.

"Arriving at the jail is as much a mystery to me as you. All I remember is guards hauling me away from Eric, and then I woke up in a cell." I stopped and took a few breaths, "I prayed to anyone that would listen, and a Goddess came to my aid."

"Oh, barnacles, they are always in it for themselves. What did you agree to do?" Sebastian raises his crabby brow.

"A little avenging of her family line. That's all." I smile weakly.

"Come now, Ari. I wasn't hatched yesterday. This is very bad. What would your father say?" Sebastian asks.

"My father has nothing to do with this. I'm no longer part of his kingdom. Besides, I'm a grown woman now! I can make my own decisions." I straighten my shoulders.

"That may be, but I don't believe the King would've left you there. I heard almost all the land gossip first, and I came for you as fast as my legs could carry me. You may live on land but always have family under the sea. So, I ask again, what did you promise her?"

I was just about to spill my guts to my friends when the sounds of dying animals echoed off the cave walls.

"Scuttle, you found me."

"Heyya, Kid, of course I did. I have some great news, too. A sea lion told me, a whale told him, a dolphin told him there was a tracker that works both onshore and at sea, not too far from this cave. He should be able to help you find who is responsible for the death of Eric. You just exit the cave and follow the coast south until there is a fork in your path. Then you head west, and you'll run right into his cottage. Or was it east? No, it was definitely west,." Scuttle puts a wing to his beak. "Anyway, It's the only one with a metal rooster on the roof."

"Oh, thank you, Scuttle. I'll head out at first light. I didn't get much rest last night between the snores of the jailer and the creaks of my cot," I tell them with a yawn. The sounds of the ocean always seem to calm me, even on my worst days.

"Get some rest, kiddo. If you need any more help, just call for me, and I'll fly in to save the day."

"I know you will, thank you."

Scuttle starts his eerie song once again as he heads out of the mouth of the cave, leaving me with Flounder and Sebastian still waiting for an explanation.

"The Goddess needs my help with some vengeance, and she will aid me in finding the people who did this to Eric. It's no worse than what I agreed with the Sea Witch."

"I don't like this one bit, Ari." Sebastian crosses his claws.

"Yeah, me neither," Flounder pipes up.

"Well, it's too late to go back now. I already agreed

SINGING DAGGER

to it. If it wasn't for the Goddess, I'd still be rotting in a human prison. Are you going to help me or not?" Both Flounder and Sebastian sigh. "Good, then we leave at first light to find this tracker." I turn away, satisfied for now.

With my first plan settled, I move farther from the shoreline, hoping to get the rest I need. After making a bed of sorts, I wrap my arms around the purse and pull it tight to my chest before turning toward the cave wall to sleep. There's no way I'll lose the instrument that'll help me get my revenge.

ARI

Everything hurts when I wake, I'm not accustomed to sleeping on the hard ground. With a tinge of sadness, I reflect on the luxury I've lived in during the last year. Stretching my arms, I sit up. The bag with the dagger rolls into my lap, and the handle peeks out. A thrill rushes through my veins as I run my finger along the hilt.

"*Vengeance*," it hisses, and my cheeks flame with need. Soon, we will be on our way.

I finger-comb through my hair, hatching a plan for the day. Before we leave, I'll need a disguise. Standing, I walk over to the many trunks of human items. Scuttle and I have found over the year. In one, I see black pants and a top that will suffice. All I need are boots. Digging around some more, I find what I need and quickly dress. Deciding on discretion, I also tie a scarf around my head to hide my signature red locks. As the finishing touch, I pull the purse back over my head and walk toward the water.

"Oh no, I'll need money," I exclaim, doubling back.

Rummaging around, I grab anything small and shiny—adding the booty to my bag.

"Sebastian," I call, "are you ready?"

"Yes, Ari." His legs clatter along the rocks toward me. Flounder peeks up from the water, and I wave. "You're going to have to stay behind, find Scuttle, will you?" Flounder nods and waves a fin before disappearing into the water.

In one motion, I bend down, scoop up the little crab, and place him in the purse with the dagger. He grouches a little before settling into position. Thankfully, he's used to me toting him around. Repeating Scuttle's odd directions in my head, I step out of the cave and begin my trek along the beach.

The sun glitters off the water as I follow the narrow path. Above me, birds nesting on the cliffside chatter. Intent on my mission, I swing my hand as I progress forward. The sand is packed enough that the walk is easy and goes by fast. Before I know it, I've come to the first marker—a fork in the trail. Turning west, I continue.

"Ari," Sebastian peeks from the bag, "are you sure I can't convince you to seek help from your father?"

"Sebastian, you know he will only want to destroy the town. I can't be responsible for that." I frown. "This is going to work, trust me."

I can feel Sebastian staring at me, but I focus on the emerging town instead. I've never ventured south of the cave as the palace is just north of the entrance. Little houses begin popping up on the road above me, with people working in the gardens or sitting on the stoops. I wave, and most wave back—although there are a few whispers as I pass, which makes my skin crawl.

I spot the cottage Scuttle mentioned when the sun is a quarter of the way in its daily path. On its roof, a black rooster spins with the wind. Stage fright grips me as I ponder what I might say to the man inside. I don't even know his name! Stepping up to the mat, I stall. Before I can work it all out, the door opens, and a man with a brown hat and a coil of rope thrown across his shoulder steps out, almost colliding with me.

"Oh, sorry about that! I wasn't expecting any visitors!" The man grabs me by the arm to keep me from falling back.

"It's my fault. I was trying to think of how to knock," I bite my lip.

The man chuckles, looking into my eyes. "Knocking's the easy part; it's the talking part that gets me." He shrugs.

At ease, I smile back. "Indeed. I was told you're a tracker?"

"That's the word on the streets," he grins. "What does a young lady such as yourself need a tracker for?"

I look around and notice some neighbors gawking. Closing the flap on my bag, I move to the cottage's interior. "I'd rather not say out here if you don't mind?"

The man looks up at a small crowd gathered on the road. "Yeah, sure, come on in. My name's Storm, by the way." He motions for me to take the lead.

"Ari," I state as I cross the threshold. Sebastian rustles around in the bag, but I hold the flap closed.

He's probably due some water after this chat. Too bad my magic dagger can't help him become a land creature at will.

The door closes, and I reach the middle of the one-roomed cottage. Not sure where to sit, I look around. Storm points to two chairs near the window, and I oblige. Now the tricky part comes, deciding how much to tell him about my plight.

"Back to the tracking. What or who do you need found?" Storm sets the rope at his feet.

Deciding whether it's sink or swim, I take a deep breath. "It's complicated. I'm being accused of a crime I didn't commit. I need you to help me find the perpetrators while also helping me hide from those who would see me die." I stare into his eyes, willing him to help me. Storm doesn't flinch, but his mouth falls open as he begins to really look at me. In one quick movement, he stands and crosses the room.

"I can pay you." I rise, sinking my hand into the purse. The dagger warms at my touch, but I pass it up and pull out a string of pearls.

"Listen ... Princess? If that's who you are, it's not about money. What you're asking is dangerous, to say the least. Where would we even start if I decide to help you?"

Kicking the chair over, I take a deep breath. I need this man to help me. I still don't know enough about the humans to enact vengeance on my own. *If only there were some magic I could use to force him to my will.* I pace the small space.

"You surely have ears around town; there must be

some rumors, some leads as to who really did this to Eric. Where would you normally start on a case to find a person or belonging?"

"I can take a trip to the tavern. Lots of drunks and idiots in there. Someone is bound to slip up and let a juicy, little secret loose. It might be best if you were to remain here. If you're in hiding, we'd better not risk taking you to the busiest part of town."

"Go," the dagger whispers to me.

"If you have a spare cloak, I can use that as a disguise. I'd like to see this tavern, and a drink is just what I need right about now."

The human drinks they serve at these places may be just what I need to help get my mind off my husband. The flashbacks of him are shaking me to my core, and the more frequent they become, the sicker my stomach becomes.

"It's your neck," the tracker states as he throws me a cloak.

I pull it around my head and shoulders, taking care to tuck in all of my hair. Both as a mermaid and now as a human, it's rare to have fiery red hair, so it's hard not to be seen.

"Ready, my lady?" Storm asks with a crooked smile.

I take a minute to look at the man for the first time since walking up to his house. He's handsome, but I shouldn't think of that now. I'm wanted for my husband's murder. If I get caught, it won't be because I shacked up with some pretty face.

"The question is more like, are *you* ready? This was my idea." I sigh.

Confusion crosses Storm's face.

"Well then, let's go. If you are nice enough, I'll let you buy me a drink," I say as I follow Storm toward the door.

The puckered expression on his face leads me to believe he's still trying to work out my words. He better be more than a good-looking man, or I'll be eating a seagull for dinner.

"How long have you lived in this town?" I almost gag on my words. I hate small talk.

"My whole life. My father was a tracker, as was his father before him. This town never ceases to require my skills, it's a win-win."

"What are your skills? I know you're a tracker, but that doesn't tell me much about what you do."

"I'm the guy you come to if you lose something or someone. Normally, it's just a case of a drunk not coming home, which usually means they are sleeping in a barn. But if it's lost, I can find it."

Gods, I was going to have to kill Scuttle for this. He sent me to a man that locates drunks. How was this man going to be helpful in my quest for vengeance?

"Trust him," the dagger whispers again.

Seriously, this piece of metal is trying to tell me that he will help on my quest, too? This shit is getting fucked up.

"Just the man I need, then," I fake a smile as best as I can.

With a shrug, Storm leads me out the door and up to the main road. He doesn't say much until we stand in front of a dump.

"Here we are, The Sea Shanty." Storm tips his hat.

"Charming," I groan.

Storm pulls the door open just as a drunken man stumbles out. "Thank you, Sir," the man slurs and bumbles down the road. Storm motions for me to go ahead of him, and I'm a little reluctant, but I do. I tighten my grip on my bag and head for the empty table at the back in the shadows. Not wanting my back to the crowd, I take the chair against the wall. This way, I can people-watch while Storm does his thing.

As I scan the room, a beautiful lady drops a bright-blue, bubbling drink off at my table with a smile. "From the gentleman at the bar."

I glance past her and note that the drink is from Storm. I say thank you to both of them at once, and I breathe a little easier, knowing I don't have to insult some asshole.

Storm starts to chat up the bartender, and I go back to people-watching.

I sip the blue drink when Sebastian starts to wiggle in my bag. Pulling my load into my lap, the flap falls back, and my crabby, little friend stares at me.

"Where are we, Ari?"

"With the tracker, trying to get a lead or a crumb on who could've done this. I haven't been human that long, but it seems as if I have a few enemies already. Get back down. Once I have more information, I'll clue you in. I can't be seen talking to a crab."

Sebastian starts to protest but does as I ask and just in time. Storm joins me.

"There is some talk about you and the murder of

Prince Eric. The chatter on you is not nice. What did you do for all this hatred?"

"Umm, let's see. Saved the prince from drowning, killed a sea witch, married said prince, and now we're here."

"So, the rumors were true, then. I have some questions for you, but there will be time for that later."

"Did you get anything useful? Or was all the gossip about me?"

"Mostly you, but there was a little chatter about a couple of princesses in the area. They are staying at the inn, I have a contact there I can visit, and she'll spill the beans on them. She kinda has a little thing for me." Storm spreads his lips into a cheesy grin that almost makes me gag.

"Oh, I don't want you to do anything that will make you uncomfortable." I stuff Sebastian into my bag.

"Nah, she's a sweet girl. We could get you a room at the inn. That is unless you plan on going back to the castle?"

"Yeah, no. That will be the last place I will be going. I like my head right where it is. A good night's sleep will be a welcome change from the last few days."

"If you're ready, we can head there now," Storm drains the drink in his hand.

"I am," I say as I take one last swig of my drink.

After Storm stands, he holds an elbow out for me, and I take it.

We are almost out the door when someone runs up behind us and snatches my bag.

"Stop, thief!" I yell. I'm not too good on my feet.

Taking after him on these things would only call for a rolled ankle or worse.

Storm unhooks from me and starts after the person. He has some speed; I'll give him that. The two of them disappear around a corner. I stand there like an idiot waiting for Storm to return.

STORM

My feet pound against the ground as I chase the man who took Ari's bag. The asshole smells like a dead fish even from this far back, so it's not like he can hide. I'm just hoping he figures that part out before I have to chase him too far.

"Not sure why you keep running!" I yell. "I'm going to catch you."

The thief turns his head to reply, which winds up being his undoing because he slams into my buddy, Wendell, as he steps around the corner. Wendell, being the perpetual jokester, stands on the man's back and strikes a pose.

"Looks like you'll be needing to answer to Storm," Wendell looks down at the man, pressing his boot against the back of his head.

A muffled answer is all the thief can muster considering his position. Seeing as Wendell has a handle on the grub, I slow down to catch my breath. To our utter amazement, he gets a second wind and heaves his body upward. Wendell loses his balance, falling on the ground. The man springs up, bag clutched to his belly.

"Get the bag!" I scream.

A scuffle between the two begins. Wendell grabs the man's belt with one hand and the purse with another. Joining the fray, I swipe the guy's legs from under him. As he falls, the purse rips, emptying its contents on the cobblestones. The thief looks from Wendell to me before scrambling to his feet and taking off.

Annoyed, I squat down and begin scooping the contents back into the now almost useless bag. There's jewelry, a few forks and a beautiful dagger scattered at Wendell's feet. My hand is on the dagger when a little crab crawls out and begins snapping his claws at me. I sit back on my heels, staring at the angry crustacean in confusion. I may be imagining things, but I could swear the dagger whispered something.

"Storm, is there something you want to tell me? Did you join a rival ship?" Wendell scoops the crab up without injury, bringing me back to reality.

"What?" I shake my head, realizing the contents of Ari's bag look like booty. "No, Wend, if I changed my mind about being a pirate—you'd be the first to know. This purse belongs to my client."

"Oh thank goodness." Ari rushes up to the both of us before I can say anything more. She grabs the dagger from my hand and tucks it into her belt before taking the crab into her hands. "Sebastian, are you okay?" She brings the crustacean to her face. Wendell and I share a confused look when the crab turns its back toward her.

"Where's my purse? I've got to get Mr. Grumpy Shell into some water," Ari looks around.

"I'm afraid your purse is ruined, but you may have

my bag." Wendell unstraps his from his side, offering it to her with a wink. "It's empty, as I lost my last coins at the gambling table just before I ran into Storm and the would-be thief.

Ari raises an eyebrow, but takes the offered bag. As she clasps the strap, Wendell and I retrieve the rest of the contents for her. She places everything in her new bag quietly as we watch. I can't help but stare at her, and it doesn't escape my notice that my friend hasn't looked away either.

"Thank you for the bag." Ari scrunches her nose. "I'm sorry I didn't catch your name."

Wendell straightens his posture and smiles, gold tooth gleaming. "Wendell of the Jolly Barnacle, it's my pleasure. You must be Storm's new client, what is it you've lost?"

Ari smiles so big that her eyes light up and I find myself a little jealous she didn't look at me in the same way. Feeling protective for some reason, I clear my throat. "Ahem, this is Ari, she's asked me to find some people for her." I step to her side.

"You mean that guy?" Wendell points to the thief who is still scrambling down the road.

Ari frowns at the thief and shakes her head. "No, that guy is just a random jerk. The ones I seek are far more dangerous."

"Come join us for a drink," Ari points to the inn. "You can keep me company while Storm works his magic, gathering a bit more information and procuring me a room. Lead on, Storm?"

Pinching my lips, I nod. Of course, she invited the

pirate, he's good with the ladies. Why do I even care? Trying to sort out my head, I escort the two of them down the block toward the inn. This side of Tirulia is known for its rough edges, but it's also a more close-knit community since mostly everyone works in a trade that lends to the other. There's one tavern, The Siren, and one inn, The Quiet Harpy, which are connected among the shops and cottages.

The wooden sign for The Quiet Harpy flaps in the breeze as we approach. Dark skies warn of a storm approaching. Pulling my coat closed, I step up and open the door. Moving to the side to allow Ari to enter first, I give Wendell the stink eye. On most occasions, I enjoy his company—but I usually work alone. At least that's why I'm telling myself I want him to leave.

"Welcome to the South Side's finest establishment." Wendell steps up beside Ari, waving his hand with a flourish.

"It's nothing compared to what she's accustomed to," I grouch, thinking how large the palace must be from the inside.

Ari turns to face me. "Don't be a guppy, this is fantastic. I've never been on the South Side before," she smiles and my insides go a little gooey.

"Right, well, take a seat and order what you like. I'll go talk to Samantha to see what I can find out," I stutter, leaving them abruptly.

Damn Wendell and his charming smile, Ari was almost like putty in his hands. *Get it together, Storm, why do you even care? She's a client and on the run for murder, not the type of woman you need in your life.*

The inn is hopping today, which isn't normal. I clench my satchel close as I push past all the people milling around the check-in desk. The beauty behind the counter looks a little flustered, but once I catch her eye, she relaxes a little.

"Heya, handsome. What can I do for you?"

I have to turn on the charm. I've been struggling a little since Ari smiled at Wendell. But I have to push that aside and get Ari a room and the dirt on her husband's murderer or murderers.

"I need a room for a cousin and with a side of information." I lean against the counter.

"I didn't know you had family." Samantha bats her eyelashes.

I raise an eyebrow at her. "Do you know a lot about me?"

"I'm learning there is more than meets the eye." She winks. "You're in luck, I have one room left."

"I'll take it." I smile at her.

She dangles the key in front of my face. "But it will cost you double."

"Ah, why you gotta do me like that?" A grimace crosses my face at her words.

"We're in demand, gotta take advantage when I can." She chuckles with a shrug.

"Fair enough, I'll take it. My place is too small for a guest. But I want some information. Why are all these people here?"

"Well, you've heard the news about Prince Eric? Who am I kidding? Of course, you have. The word on the street is that the prime suspect, that strange princess, somehow escaped and now there is a hefty bounty on her head. I just knew he shouldn't have married a foreigner! Anyway, all the hunters are here to try and cash in on it. As if the princess would be stupid enough to stay in town. If I was accused of killing my husband, my ass would be long gone."

"Huh, I knew about Eric but not that his wife did it. Are they sure it was her?" I look back over my shoulder but can't find where Ari and Wendell have sat, the space between the tavern and the check-in is filled with people.

"She was caught in the room with his bleeding body, all signs point to her." Samantha leans into me. Just as I'm about to ask her another question, there's a big ruckus at the front door that demands our attention.

"Oh great, they're back again." Samantha sighs as her eyes glance at the men coming in the door.

Samantha hands me the key, "Stay put, this won't take long."

Three burly men cut through the people still milling around, not caring that they knocked a few older people down on their way to the desk. Someone needs to teach them a lesson. Not me, but somebody else. They are on the giant side of men and I'm taller than most. I can't confront them and risk Ari getting thrown in the mix. So, I step to the end of the desk to make room for the leader of the three.

"Three rooms," the first one grunts out, pounding a fist on the rickety desk.

"Sorry, fellas, the last room has been taken. We are

all full up," Samantha says plainly as if she's not intimidated by him in the least.

"Check again, this will not please our employers," another huffs, blowing his curly hair from in front of his piercing, blue eyes.

"Well, I'm the only inn on the south side, and business is good. I just rented the last room out a few minutes ago. We are full up, I guess you should have come in a little earlier."

Samantha throws a smirk in my direction. I return it but she is playing a dangerous game with these guys.

The three men don't seem to notice her smile in my direction and exit as loudly as they came. Not until they disappear through the door do I breathe a little easier. Most of the people in here wouldn't realize that Ari was the woman they were looking for but those men looked like personal guards for royalty. They wouldn't overlook her red hair, hood on or not.

"They sure were pleasant." I scrunch my nose.

"Yeah, they left a lot quieter than I expected. There are some princesses visiting our little shithole, which makes no sense as they usually stay on the north side. The worst part is they keep sending their guards to reserve rooms, but then they don't stay and I'm out the coin."

"Why would they do that?"

"They are rich, who knows why they do what they do?" Samantha throws up her hands. "Now, how many nights is your cousin staying?"

I unload a pile of coins onto the desk, the clinking drawing too many eyes in our direction. "A week for now. If I need the room for more nights, I'll make sure to give you a warning before checkout."

"Thanks, sweetie. Once you get your cousin settled, want to meet me for a drink at The Siren?" Samantha straightens her apron, smiling.

As much as I want to decline, I know she may have more information I can use to help Ari. "You got it, but you took all my coins, so it will be on your dime."

"It's a deal." Samantha laughs. "I'll be over there within the hour."

"As will I," I promise.

Swerving through the bodies, I make my way back to Ari and Wendell. They're deep in conversation and extremely close. My cheeks flame with anger, but I stamp it back down. *She's not mine*, I remind myself.

"Got you a room, the last one." I jingle the key in my hand much like Samantha did to me just minutes earlier.

"That was lucky. Wendell, here, just offered to let me stay on his ship if you were unsuccessful." Ari pats Wendell on the arm, another move that makes me bothered.

"Um, hum. I'm sure he did. I've been on his ship, you'd be bunking with him and his shipmates. By all means, if it's a pirate's life for you, go with Wendell," I say with more heat than I meant.

"What's gotten into you, Storm? Do I need to order you a drink?" Wendell asks, raising an eyebrow.

"The last thing I need is a drink that ends in a bar fight," I glare at the pirate. Too many times has that been my fortune while hanging out with him. "Ari, let's get you to your room. I have a date with Samantha. Hopefully, she can give me some more juicy tidbits."

"She is a looker, but you have a beauty right here. Why would you pick her over Ari?" Wendell jibes.

"Ari is a client. I need information to help her. How else do you suggest I get that for her?" I grit out.

"Smart thinking. There are so many people here. It may be best to hide in my room until this place clears out some. Too many eyes and too many chances to get caught." Ari's eyes scan the room warily.

Offering a hand toward Ari, I stand "If you will, my lady."

The smile on her face has my temperature rising. *Calm down, Storm. She is a client.* I try my best to gather my wits before we exit the room.

"I'll see you later, Wendell. It was nice to meet you," Ari states as she takes my hand.

"If you're ever at the dock, look me up." Wendell raises his glass. "And, Ari, I might mention that I know a blacksmith that can help you clean up that precious dagger of yours. A piece like that should be treasured." He winks.

"If we need a dingy, I'll be sure to bring her your way." I smirk at Wendell.

Before he can reply again, I wrap my fingers around Ari's and hold tight. The room is filling up by the minute. Pushing through the crowd, we cross into the inn. Just past the desk where Samantha talks with another burly customer, we ascend the stairs to the second floor.

ARI

Ever since I woke up in that damned cell, I've felt off. Add the dagger and now two men to the mixture and I'm positively spinning. Storm casually telling us he had a "date" with Samantha rubs me in all the wrong places, and I have no excuse for feeling as I do. The love of my live was murdered and here I am drooling over two strangers. I need to remember my mission.

I'm so lost in thought, I don't realize that we've come to my door. Storm stands holding the door open, a quizzical look on his face. "I hope this will do?"

Absently, I wave him off and enter the room before realizing how rude my actions were. I'm certainly not myself these days, Moryana wasn't kidding. Embarrassed, I turn around, catching him as he begins descending the stairs.

"Storm, wait!" I call. "Would you come in for a moment, please?"

Storm gives me a long look before shrugging and coming back up the steps. Once he crosses the threshold, I close the door. There's another awkward

SINGING DAGGER

moment as we bump into each other before he settles into the side chair and I sit on the bed, unstrap the bag and set it beside me. At that moment, Sebastian throws open the flap of my bag and clacks his claw at me, "Ari, I need water!"

"Oh right." I look around and spot the water basin. Tipping the jug beside it, I fill the bowl before plopping my friend inside. When I turn back to Storm, his jaw is open.

"I heard the stories that you were a ... but I didn't," he stutters, staring at me.

I blow a stray piece of hair from my face before pacing in front of him. There's so much to say, and yet I'm not sure how far I can trust Storm. If only I were better at being a person; with Eric, I never had to try very hard, things were just easy. How I miss him.

"I know this is a lot," I finally manage. "Before I tell you my entire story, I need to know I can trust you. Will you swear on my dagger to help me on this quest?"

Storm scratches the back of his neck. "I don't see how that will make you trust me any more than the fact that I could have turned you in downstairs for a heavy bounty, but sure."

He's got a point, but there's something deep in me that needs him to make the pledge. Crossing back to the bed, I open the bag and pull out the dagger. The ruby shimmers in the low light of the room, almost pulsing along with the rhythm of my heart. Clasping the hilt, I raise the blade in front of my face. Small details I hadn't noticed before catch my eye. The cross guards are gold with two seashells in the center facing outward with a pearl in the center. A beautiful etching of a shell also graces the blade. Everything about the weapon calls to me. The more I gaze, the brighter the ruby flares.

"Ari?" Storm taps my shoulder. "You seemed lost for a moment."

Facing him, I fake a smile. "Sorry, I haven't had this dagger long and I was admiring the craftsmanship that was put into it." Holding it out, blade in one hand and hilt in the other I search Storm's eyes. "Swear on the Singing Dagger that you will join my quest and never betray me, unto the pain of death." I hum my signature tune and the dagger warms.

Storm's hand hovers over the dagger. He regards me with a shiver of fear, or maybe excitement, before he settles his palm over the hilt. "I swear to assist you, Ari, in your pursuit and never to betray you. If I do, may the pain of death take me into the seas."

A red glow emits from the dagger, and it whispers, "So let it be."

Storm snatches back his hand, holding it against his chest. "Okay, now explain. Everything, Ari, After that little show, I need to know exactly what is going on."

Keeping my eyes on his, I sit on the bed. Storm follows suit, pulling the chair opposite me so that our knees are almost touching. After a deep breath, I fold my hands and begin.

"The stories of my beginning are all true. I know the palace tried to cover up the fact that I was once a mermaid by spinning a tale of a foreign princess come to Tirulia, but the truth is I rescued Eric during a storm at sea. Having fallen in love with him, I made an agreement with a sea witch to help me become human. Long story short, she tricked me and I almost lost my soul. In the end, my father King Triton, gave into my wish and granted me legs. Since then, Eric and I have been living happily. That is until two nights ago. Eric was murdered and I was framed. My memory of the night is hazy, but I know I would never do such a thing. When I was in my cell, a Goddess visited me and gave me this dagger." I hold the weapon between us. "It's magical. She told me that when I sing, it will help guide me. I'm still learning how to use it." I stop, trying to gauge his reaction.

"And the crab?" Storm points.

"That's Sebastian. He is part of my father's court. I can talk to any sea creature." I shrug.

Storm leans forward, elbows on his knees and face braced in his hands. Part of me wants to comfort him somehow, but I know he'll have to come to terms with everything before we can move forward. Giving him space, I stand to check on Sebastian. The look on his little crustacean face is disapproving, but that's his baseline.

"Do you have other questions?" I ask as I scoop up the crab for a moment.

"I ... don't know. My head is spinning and my heart is thudding like a galloping horse," Storm whispers. "If the dagger is magical, why do you need me?"

"Good question. The dagger will only activate when I am near the subject I am seeking. I'm sure like anything magical, there is more than one catch—but that's the main one. I have to work to seek my answers, the dagger is merely a tool." I shrug.

"Okay. We'll need to plan our next move. I can't think right now, so I'm going to go downstairs and meet with Samantha as planned. I need a drink, or two. Once I pump her for information, I'll come back—okay?" He looks up, worry lines marring his otherwise handsome countenance.

A lump forms in my throat at the thought of him leaving, but I nod. "Yes, of course. Take the time you need."

I hate for him to leave on that note but I won't stop him. It's a lot to take in; if I was in his shoes would I think I was just a crazy person? I mean when I was little, I never believed all the stories of the land walkers, that was until I found some of their things out on a swim. It's what started my obsession and collection of all things land lovers.

The door clicks when Storm closes the door behind him and I fling myself back on the bed. The springs on the bed creak under my weight.

"Ari, none of that. We have to figure out who did this to Eric and get your name cleared. You know your father would take you back and protect you from these land walkers," Sebastian's voice is an octave lower than usual.

I turn my head toward the water basin where I had placed my little, red friend. "I'm not going to hide in the ocean. There are some things that my father can't save me from. When I prayed for help, he didn't rescue me. He left me in my cell until Moryana came and I was free. So no, I will not be running to Daddy to fix this. I was given the tools I need to do it myself and now I have Storm as well. I can do this."

"Ari…" there is a warning in his tone.

"If you aren't going to help, just run back and tell my father. You were always good at that."

Sebastian's face falls. "That's not what I meant, I just know hell or sea water he would drown this land to keep you safe."

"That may be but I can't run to him because there is a problem in my life. I chose Eric over my father and my life in the water. This is something I have to figure out for myself."

My little, crabby friend retreats back into the water and I think he got the hint that I wasn't going to take his advice. I roll over until I'm facedown on the bed and let out a scream. It's nice to just let go for once.

After I'm all screamed out, I get up and take in the little room. For being on the tough end of town, it's not as worn down or dirty as one might think it would be. My eyes scan the room until they stop on the little mirror above where Sebastian is in the water. The ink on my face is just above my eyebrow, some sort of filigree and I'm still confused as to why it appeared. I would think I would remember sitting to have this put on my face. When I run a finger over the black ink, it's smooth to the touch, so it would have to be magic or something else. There is no way a tattoo like this would just heal the moment it was placed.

"So weird," I mutter to myself, then I notice my hair.

The hood I was using to cover it has it all over the place.

I go back to my new bag that Wendell was nice enough to give me since he and Storm ripped up my other one. Well, really it was the thief's fault, if he hadn't snatched it off my shoulder, I would have my bag. I take a moment to inspect the bag, this one is better made then the one I started with and I have hope that it will outlast a thief if that happens again. Being on the Southside, I can see it happening again.

I dig in the depth until I find my dinglehopper and start to tame my flaming locks. Deciding it's best to tie it back, my fingers braid three strands together like the maid at the palace had shown me.

"I'm digging that new hair style," Storm states from the doorway. A little hiccup escapes from his lips and he smiles at me.

How did he sneak up on me? And how many drinks did he consume? He staggers in and sways as he takes a seat in the chair once more. But he nearly missed and landed on the floor.

"Are you alright?" I ask.

"Of course. Samantha thought shots were a good idea." He smirks.

"Clearly, you can't hold your liquor as well as you think. How are we going to seek out those that did this to my husband if you can't even stand? You took an oath to help me and in your current state, I don't see how you will manage that."

"I'm fine," he slurs with a dismissive wave. "Did you hear me when I came back?"

"No, but I was lost in my own thoughts. Your steps to the chair were like a herd of elephants. We don't need to attract the attention of the whole Southside after dark. If we did, why not go out in daylight or wear a bell and say 'here's the princess you're looking for.' If you aren't going to be any help, I guess I'll go to the docks and find Wendell. At least he's a pirate and they can function drunk or not."

At the mention of the pirate's name, Storm frowns but seems to sober up some.

"So, you don't think people will dismiss a drunk that passes out near them and continue their chattering? I had two drinks with Samantha, she—on the other hand—could drink your precious Wendell under the table without even batting an eye. But she did tell me to seek out the guards that came to the inn earlier, she believes that they are up to something. Why else reserve a room and never use it? There is something going on here and I'll get down to the bottom of it," he promises as his face comes closer to mine.

"So, this was all a charade to raise my temper? Well, you've succeeded, Tracker."

ARI

Human or merman, all males seem to be infuriating. Avoiding looking at Storm, I stand and begin to sort through the items in my bag. I really shouldn't walk around with everything I own strapped to my side. By the click of his heels, he's pacing the room behind me. Sighing heavily, I turn to Sebastian.

"Bast, can you wait here for now? I don't know how long we'll be out and I don't want you to dry." His little, crabby lips purse, but he nods his head. "Be careful, Ari."

Settling on a few coins and the dagger, I stuff everything else under the mattress of the bed. I'm impressed with the quality of the bag Wendell gifted me. The leather is soft and supple as I strap it to my side. Unable to help myself, I lift the flap and touch the dagger. I'm hesitant to try using it as a beacon, as Moryana instructed; something about being led around by the weapon feels strange.

"You know, your jewels would be safer if you lifted a floorboard up, everyone stuffs valuables under their

SINGING DAGGER

beds." Storm steps into my vision.

Pinching my lips together, I cross the room and kneel under the window. Storm has a good point, so I grab the dagger and pry up the loosest board near the wall. Before I can rise to grab my stuff, Storm is by my side, his hands full. Our hands meet and my cheeks flame. Chancing a glance up, I lock eyes with him.

"Thank you," I manage before tearing my gaze away and stowing the treasures.

Storm tugs at his collar. "For what it's worth, I didn't mean to upset you."

Breathing a little easier, I smile. "Let's start this evening over. Are you ready for some spying?"

"The better question is, are you ready, Princess? I don't mean to be rude, but how much experience do you have beyond the castle?"

Placing one hand on my hip, and using the other to point the dagger at Storm, I curl my lip. "If you think I'm some delicate flower, you've got another thing coming. You land-walkers have it so easy, I spent most of my life running from sharks and fisherman's hooks." My chest throbs as I push the blade into Storm's chest. "There's nothing that you can say to keep me from hunting down Eric's killers. I've asked for your help, but I will just as happily work alone."

Storm rubs a hand over his face. "Aye, I hear you, Ari. Forgive me for my blunder, " his voice lowers to an almost whisper, "it's just I'm not used to working with royalty and all. You make me nervous."

A hive of bees would be quieter than the noise in my head right now. It's not Storm's fault that I'm in this position, or that people seem to constantly underestimate me. Nevertheless, I find myself heated beyond control. If I don't rein myself in, I'm going to explode. Clenching the dagger at my chest, I face the wall in an attempt to cool down.

"Ari." Storm gently touches my shoulder, guiding me toward him. Without thinking, I bury my face in his chest as tears flow down my cheeks. To his credit, Storm doesn't flinch, he wraps his arms around me. Some strong princess I am, openly weeping in a stranger's hold. Except Storm isn't a stranger anymore, is he? The dagger warms in my hold and I take a deep breath.

"I'm sorry," I sniff. "It's been a rough few days."

Storm lifts my chin. Our eyes meet and in the stillness, my heartbeat slows. The sounds of the inn drift away and I take a deep breath. I can't help but notice how Storm's gaze lingers on my lips. The dagger pulses in my grip, almost pushing me closer to the tracker. The static between us arcs, triggering a flush of heat in my chest.

"We should go," I whisper, before our lips meet.

The clatter of a chamberpot being dropped echoes through the hall and we separate slightly. Just like that, whatever moment we would have had is gone. Storm clears his throat as he steps away from me. "Yes, you're right. Might I suggest you tie up your hair before we set out? It's a beautiful shade of red, but it stands out like a sore thumb," he reaches around his neck and unties his scarf, handing it over to me.

Our fingers linger a moment before I take the black

fabric. After stowing the dagger away, I wrap the scarf around my head, tying a knot at the nape of my neck like I've seen so many of the maids do at the palace. When I look up to check the mirror, Storm's gaze catches mine from over my shoulder. The more I'm drawn to him, the more guilt settles in my gut like a load of rocks. I know part of the feelings I'm having derive from feeling so alone, but I've also got a sneaking suspicion the dagger is also playing a part in them. Confused, I lock them down for the moment and turn toward Storm.

"Ready?"

He nods, grabs his own bag from the table and opens the door for us. Straightening my shoulders, I walk past him and wait as he locks the door. He places a hand at my waist, and we descend the stairs together.

"We'll take a midnight stroll at the docks," Storm leans in, whispering. "From there, we'll be able to get a good look at these guards. Heck, maybe our best bet is to find a perch on the Jolly Barnacle, Wendell's ship. That way we won't raise any suspicions traipsing around."

His plan seems solid. From my old habit of walking the beach at night, I'm aware that the best place for watching men at their dice and drinks is down by the docks. Once we figure out who the guards in question are, we can follow them. Too bad Scuttle is so loud and clumsy; otherwise, I'd seek his help as well.

I have Storm with me, but it doesn't stop the loneliness creeping up. However, none of my friends were made for land living and the one person I had was murdered. *No time to be mopey, Ari, you have a killer or killers to find.*

Storm bounces down each step as I take care. I'm grateful to not have had more drinks with Wendell earlier.

"Where is it that we are headed?" I ask as I continue down.

He doesn't reply until I hit the landing next to him.

"Well, you and Wendell hit it off so well, and the pier is a great place to people-watch, so I thought that's where we would head."

"Smart, I bet a lot of people walk by there and have loose lips. No offense to Wendell but I don't think the most savvy people hang out there."

This gets a little chuckle from Storm. "You aren't wrong there, Ari. The docks aren't a current hangout for the rich, even the ones that own the ships won't slum there," Storm says as he holds the door open for me to exit.

"My father always warned us about fishermen and their hooks. Maybe I'm just biased because of his words." I shrug as I walk out into the night air.

The scent of the sea hits my nose and I feel more at home here even being on land.

"I love that smell. The salt of the sea always soothes me, I think that's why I like my cottage so much. Just the right mix of land and water." Storm takes a deep breath.

Sounds like the palace. Eric wanted to move into a little cottage further in the woods for some privacy, but

I insisted that we stay. If only we did as he wanted, maybe I wouldn't be here but in his arms right now.

"Ari, this way," Storm states, waving his arms to the left.

"Sorry, the scent just brought back some memories," I say as I head in the direction he wants to go.

The sun hasn't quite set and the road is dimming with each step.

"Hey, beautiful, you looking for a good time?" a voice in the dark hollers toward me.

Storm, who was walking a few steps behind yells, "Aye, this is my woman. Any of you scurvy lads try anything funny, the last thing you'll taste is the steel of my blade."

His threat ignites my core and I fan my face with my hand, hoping he doesn't notice. If he does, he doesn't mention it.

Storm takes my hand in his, pulling me away from the man whose offer he declined for me.

"I have no doubt that you could handle him yourself. But if you spilled his blood, it would've been a bitch to clean up in time to make it to Wendell's before all the drunks head home for the night," he explains, walking a little faster.

"Not a problem, I did hire you to help me. That may not have been what I meant, but it was helpful," I say as I turn to face him slightly.

I note that a smirk crosses his lips at the same moment I trip on something. If I hadn't been holding Storm's hand, I would've fallen on my face.

"What was that?" I ask as Storm glances down the alley.

"It was a foot," he states and takes a few steps closer to where the head would be. "It's the thief that stole your bag earlier."

"That's an odd coincidence. Maybe I wasn't the only one he stole from today and they weren't as nice as we were," is the only thing I can come up with.

"I suggest we get out of here fast. The last thing we need to do is get arrested for this," Storm states as he takes my hand and pulls me away from the body.

Storm didn't notice how close I got to the thief's face, but the slash across his throat was the bloodiest thing I'd ever seen. The look of surprise on his face was etched forever in my mind.

"I knew we were on the tough side of town, but are there always bodies littering the streets?" I ask as we are almost at a run.

"That is not normal. Most people would have cleaned it up already. We don't need any of the palace guards sniffing around. That is just asking for trouble," he says, not slowing his steps.

"If you move any faster, you're going to have to carry me. My legs are shorter than yours."

This gets him to slow down, "I mean I could carry you, but I didn't want you to stab me."

I laugh a little. "I promise to only do that if you deserve it, or better yet if you ask me to."

He has a bewildered look on his face, "Why would I ask you to?"

"Some people are into that." I shrug. "Are we almost

SINGING DAGGER

to the docks? It's getting harder to see with the sun going down."

"You can't hear the whiny voice of Wendell yet?" Storm asks as the first of the ships come into view.

"You really don't like him much, do you?"

"Nah, we just like to give each other shit. That is the kinda friends we are. We've known each other since we were kids. If you can't joke with them, are you even friends?" Storm asks as he ascends onto the biggest boat in the docks.

"Wendell must be a great pirate, look at this ship," I comment as I take in our surroundings. From what I can tell, all the wood is fairly new and in great shape. Not like most of the pirate ships I've seen at the bottom of the ocean.

"That I am, lass. I be the best pirate in these, here, waters," Wendell smirks from a table surrounded by candle light. He shuffles a deck of cards and pushes out a chair, gesturing for me to sit. "What be the pleasure for this visit?"

"Maybe some cards and gossip," Storm says as he takes a seat in the chair across from the pirate.

"You've come to the right place for that." Wendell's smile widens as I sit down.

ARI

The stars shine bright above and a cool breeze embraces us as we sit on the quarterdeck of the Jolly Barnacle. Wendell is persistent in his teaching me the proper terms for the parts of the beautiful ship. The sparkle in his eyes as he speaks each word gives me the feeling it's his love language, so to speak. I have to admit, his zest is infectious.

"And the mighty Kraken you see at the end of the beak is called a figurehead." Wendell puffs on his pipe. "Most ships have a bare-naked lady or mermaid—but the Jolly has a mighty beast!"

Not able to hold in a laugh, I shake my head. "I've never met a Kraken who was jolly, nor covered in barnacles."

Storm crosses his arms. "Wendell just likes to be cheeky, that's why the ship's name doesn't match the figurehead."

The two men share a look, then both pick their cards back up. The history between them is easy to see, but there's also a tightness arising that makes me sweat a bit. I'm not as innocent as I once was, I know sexual

SINGING DAGGER

tension when I feel it. Neither am I immune to the feeling, which is a bit unsettling. Sitting here drinking and playing cards with them makes my last year seem distant except for the burn in my chest to kill the murderer. I should feel guilty at my lack of grief, but I shake off the thought whilst reaching in my bag and caressing Harmony, my dagger. I figured she needed a name and can tell she is pleased by the slow vibration the hilt gives.

Shouting below catches my attention and I perk up. "Aye, let me go, I did nothing to yer!" A young ruffian struggles in the center of a group of guards. The guards wear light-blue uniforms, not the dark blue of the palace guards.

"Those might be the guards we're looking for," I whisper, pointing at a group of four men lingering beside the lamppost below the ship." Storm and Wendell sit up, both glancing without turning their heads.

One of the guards chuckles, sticks his finger into the boy's chest. "You should'na be snooping around where you're not wanted. Tell me what you heard, boy!"

"Nothing, I swear!" The youngster scrambles in the guard's hold, trying to scratch his face.

I'm surprised at how openly these men are abusing such a small boy, but when I look around at the empty pier it makes more sense. The more time I spend on land, the more I realize how different they really are up here.

I watch intently as the guards laugh at the young

boy before one of them reaches for a dagger. He grabs the boy as if he's hugging him and the boy slumps forward. Before they walk away, they drop his body in the water. I cover my mouth with my hand, surprised at how quickly it all happened. Before I can speak, Wendell has jumped up and begun shimmying down the other side of the ship.

"Wend will check on the boy. Come on, Ari, we have to follow those men!" Storm grabs me by the arm, crouching as he leads me off the ship.

By the time we make it down to the pier, there's no sight of the men. It's like they vanished into thin air. Storm and I search up and down the rows of crates to no avail. Head lowered, I slink back to the Jolly Barnacle with a sinking sensation in my stomach. There's something we aren't seeing, and I have to find out what.

One foot on the plank, I stop. Stunned that I hadn't thought of it before, I pull out the dagger. The ruby in the hilt seems to wink at me as I hold it before my face. Trying to remember Moryana's words, I began to hum. Storm steps up behind me just as Harmony begins to tug me to the left.

"This way," I whisper as I walk the pier. Step by step, I move down the wooden docks until it comes to an end. A gust of wind whips my scarf off, sending it trailing along the top of the water and out of sight. To my disappointment, Harmony becomes still and cold.

"What's going on?" Storm asks.

"I don't know. Maybe I did it wrong?" I look down at the blade in my hand. With a sigh, I place Harmony

SINGING DAGGER

back in my bag and turn to Storm. "When I sing, the dagger is supposed to help find my enemies, but all it did was bring me to the water."

Storm scratches his head. "It's possible they slipped onto a small boat and we didn't see them," he offers.

"True. Maybe they were too far away for it to work." I tap my foot. "At any rate, let's get back to the ship and see about the boy."

Storm holds out his hand and I slip mine into his grasp before walking toward the Jolly Barnacle. Waves lap against the pier, lulling my frazzled nerves. At the edge of the human world, the stars are brighter and the air smells more like home.

"I'm sorry we didn't catch up to them. I should have acted faster," Storm mumbles as we walk up the plank. "We'll get them, Ari. I promise."

Our eyes meet briefly and a flutter of wings alights in my chest. Moonlight highlights Storm's blond hair, creating a halo-like effect. For a moment, I leave everything in my life behind and take in how handsome he is. If it were any other moment, I'd lean in and kiss him right here. I'm familiar with how things work out if you leave things up to chance. But alas, the timing is terrible. Instead, I squeeze his hand and look around for Wendell.

We find the pirate in his cabin. The boy is laid on the bed, bandaged around his middle. Wendell turns as we enter, "Lucky for the kid those baddies can't aim well. Caught him in the side but missed anything important. Smart of him to act dead, though, I'd say."

"Yes, now we should let him rest. After that, we can

question him on why they did this to him," I say in a whisper.

"I know this lad and his family. They are decent people, but poor—which is likely how he got caught up in this mess. Once he's up and around, I'm sure he'll talk to me." Wendell smirks at me.

Whispering again, I say, "Keep your voice down, we don't want to wake him. He'll need his strength to heal. Let's give him some peace and talk outside."

I motion to the door and exit soon after, the two men heed my words and follow. Taking my seat at the table once again, the men do the same and Wendell grabs the deck of cards. He absentmindedly shuffles them.

"Why would the guards stab him and dump him in the sea? There is enough land-dweller stuff in the bottom, they don't need bodies in there, too," I complain and Storm gives me a warning look as if I have said too much.

"How is it that you would know that, Ari?" Wendell asks with an eyebrow raised.

"Where I'm from, there were always random objects showing up on our beaches," I say, trying to backpedal in hopes for him to drop it.

"Uh, huh. You aren't telling me the whole truth, but maybe after a few more drinks you'll open up," Wendell states as he pulls out a jug from behind his chair.

I ignore his words and press on about the boy. "So, will the boy and his family be safe or will they have to flee to somewhere new?

Storm remains silent and Wendell pulls the jug to

his lips before answering. He takes a long swig before handing it to Storm. Storm repeats what Wendell did and hands the jug toward me.

I shake my head to decline.

"That's no' very pirate-like of you," Wendell comments, taking the liquid from Storm.

"You two just drank from it and didn't even wipe the rim first," I say as my lip curls up in disgust.

That gets the two of them to hoot with laughter.

"We be pirates, there is none of that. You are handed a drink, you take it," Wendell says as he takes another drink. "The boy and his family will be fine. The guards are just lily-livered bilge rats. They do as they see fit and that boy was probably at the wrong place at the right time. Simple as that. He may have overheard something, or nothing at all. They caught him and disposed of him."

"Humans are the worst," I comment without thinking.

"Aye, now tell me, Ari. Who are you really? I may be a pirate but that doesn't make me an idiot," Wendell says as he sits forward in his chair.

"If I do that, I'll have to kill you," I say flatly without blinking.

"Do it then, either that or tell me. You're welcome to leave my ship, but I will not sit here and be lied to."

Storm starts to take up for me, but I wave him off.

"If you really want to know, then you have to do something for me first," I tell him as I slide the dagger from the satchel he gave me earlier.

"You really are going to stab me? Most women

would just show their deck cargo, that's enough to make men go stupid and forget what they were asking," Wendell says as he moves back from me.

"'Deck cargo?' Your choice of words are strange, and if I wanted to stab you, you'd already be bleeding on your wooden planks here," I say, resting the dagger on my thigh.

"Breasts, woman. You really aren't from around here, are you?"

I raise the dagger a little and wave it at him. "Do you really think it's smart to talk down to a woman that is holding something sharp? Before I can trust you, I need you to take an oath over my dagger and I'll fill you in."

"We really don't need him, Ari. Just stab him and we can go back to the hotel. This whole night has been a bust anyway," Storm pipes in.

"Aye, you'd like that, wouldn't you? Then you can just sail off with me ship."

"You two are idiots." I sigh. "I think having a pirate with a ship may be helpful in my quest. But he has to utter the oath, same as you. But if he doesn't want to, I guess I could stab him and take the ship."

Storm laughs again, but Wendell doesn't.

"What words be I needing to say?" he asks with a serious face. "You have me mixed up in this already, I best know what I be signed up for."

I tell him to hold his hand over the dagger, same as Storm did and he repeats after me. The dagger warms over my palm once again and hums in agreement that he can be trusted.

"That is the freakiest thing I've seen, and I've seen some things," he comments as he takes another drink.

"My full name is Ariel, not just Ari," I say as his eyes widen at me.

I launch into my life of woes and how I'm seeking the real killer of my husband. "The Goddess Moryana blessed me with this dagger, a blade of vengeance if you will. You two have pledged to help me on my task of revenge and clearing my name."

"If you would have led off with that, I don't think I would've taken the oath," Wendell confesses.

"That's why it was oath first, story second. If I told you and you ran off, my friend Harmony would not only help me find you, but end you. I will do whatever it takes to find out who did this to my husband," I promise, waving my dagger a little.

"Aye, can you please return that to your bag? You are waving it a little too carelessly for me. I don't want you to stab me on accident," Wendell pleads.

I raise an eyebrow at him, "If I stab you, I promise, it will be on purpose."

ARI

Wendell paces the quarterdeck, his lips moving rapidly in silent conversation with himself. A sinking feeling settles in my stomach as I watch. It may not have been my brightest idea to trick him into helping, but it was necessary. Somehow, I just know that I need him.

"He'll get over it," Storm pats my shoulder and sits down at the table.

Blowing a stray strand of hair out of my face, I take one last look at the pirate before joining Storm. Hopefully, Sebastian is okay at the inn all by himself; it's probably best if I get him back to the ocean. I don't think my crabby friend should see what comes next. He'll never understand.

Setting Harmony on the table, I trace the set of shells and pearls engraved in the cross-guard. My finger tingles when I come close to the hilt and the ruby embedded there. The red stone must be the source of magic. Inhaling, I trace the setting, wondering how I'm going to gather the courage that I'll need to kill Eric's murderer. The ruby glows and a heaviness enters my limbs. Deep in my core, change brews.

"You will be ready," Harmony whispers and a light, whirling pattern appears along the webbing between my pointer and thumb. The design matches the tattoos that appeared at my temples the night I received Harmony.

How many tattoos will appear between now and the time my quest is over? I wonder as I stare at my hand.

"Lass, tell me I'm not imagining things," Wendell leans over the table until our noses meet. My mouth falls open. A lock of his dark hair falls in his eyes, the tips touched with gold from the time he spends in the sun. Something about the deep, teak-wood color of his eyes pulls me in until I feel I'm drowning.

"Lass?" Wendell caresses my cheek, bringing me out of the trance.

"What?" I shake my head, trying to clear my thoughts.

"Did I or did I not just watch a tattoo appear on your hand?" The pirate clasps my hand in his, turning the filigree toward him.

"Hmm? Oh yes, it's Harmony. The Goddess didn't tell me about the tattoos, but they've started appearing since I received the dagger," I touch my temple absently.

Wendell draws in a breath, his hand tightening on mine. "Aye, that's deep magic. Does it hurt?" He brushes his fingers over the dark ink.

"No, but it tingles a bit when I hold Harmony," I answer.

"Blimey! For such an important weapon, you've got no proper way to carry her. At first light, we'll travel down the way to visit me ole bucko. Oli is a blacksmith, he's sure to help get her shipshape," Wendell picks up Harmony, eyeing the ruby. "Saavy?"

"Perfect," I take Harmony from his hand and stash her back in the bag for now. "I don't know about you two, but I'm exhausted. Can we call it a night?"

My heart skips a beat thinking of letting either man out of my sight. There's an unspoken question in the air as to where everyone will sleep. "I know I have a room at the inn," I twist my hands. "But I don't want to be alone. What if one of them recognized me when we checked in? Could we stay here on the Jolly Barnacle?"

Wendell and Storm both whip their heads toward me. "Yer probably right. What with the bounty on yer head and the two of you seen out and about together, it's probably best we all lay low here on me ship. After we get some shuteye, we can regroup and plan out the quest at hand. For safety, let's batten down the hatches." Wendell claps Storm on the back and they walk toward the gangplank.

Even in the dim light. I can see their muscles straining as they pull the gangplank back onto the deck. My throat tightens as I watch. As much as it pains me to admit, they're both quite handsome.

"Do you guys need help?" I ask, trying to stop staring.

"Nah, we got it," Storm says with a grunt. He sets the large beam on his shoulder and walks it back as if it weighs nothing. By the looks of either of them, I wouldn't have guessed they were so strong. I guess you can never tell what's beneath a good shirt.

"Hello?" a little voice calls from behind me. Startled, I wheel around in my chair. In the threshold of the cabin stands the boy that Wendell had bandaged up. His brown hair is tangled and hanging into his eyes and his pants have seen better days.

"Oh, you shouldn't be out of bed. That's a nasty cut you got earlier." I rush over.

"Aye, Pete. How ya doing, buddy?" Wendell asks, in a sweet tone as he makes his way over.

The little boy looks up at Wendell, eyes wide. "What happened? And why are my clothes wet?"

"You don't remember how you got that gash?" I ask in surprise.

"He lies," Harmony whispers.

"No, I was just searching for some bits of food to take back to my family. Then I woke up here," Pete scratches his head.

"Lies."

Hoping a little encouragement will change the boy's mind, I kneel. "You can tell us, Pete. We won't tell your parents what you were doing," I promise with a smile. I almost reach out to him but I don't want to freak him out any more than he already is.

He glances toward Wendell as if to get confirmation it's okay to talk.

"Pete, this is my new friend, Ari and I'm sure you know Storm. Ye be able to tell them anything, ye be able to tell me," Wendell encourages him with a wave of his hand.

"If it helps, you can pretend that Storm and I aren't even here. Just talk to Wendell directly," I offer up to Pete.

He gulps before he spins his tale, "Well, I was in the alley looking for food. It's easy pickings over by the Harpy, folks don't look twice at me. Anyway, I was near an open window when I overheard some women talking about Princess Ariel and Prince Eric. They were gloating about how their plan was working. Right then, I lost my footing and made a barrel fall over. Before I knew it, the guards started chasing me. I ran as fast as I could, but my little legs were no match for theirs. They walked me to the pier and then stabbed me."

"What made you think to act dead?" Wendell asks.

"I didn't know if they had more planned for me and I didn't want to find out. But he stuck his blade in deeper than I thought." Pete grabs his side.

"Good thinking, laddie. It's probably a good thing if you stay out of sight for a few days to be sure they won't catch up with ye. Are ye well enough to head home? I bet ya parents be worried, how bout I walk with ye?" Wendell offers Pete his hand.

Pete's eyes light up at Wendell's words. This boy must think the pirate life is a glamorous one. I won't be the one to break it to him that he couldn't be more wrong.

"That's a great idea. It was nice to meet you, Pete. Make sure you take it easy and let that wound heal," I say with a little wave.

Storm and I watch the pirate and boy lower themselves down a rope to the pier. I bet Wendell is kicking himself for not leaving the gangplank in place until the boy left, but as far as we knew he would have slept all night. I was surprised that he was up and walking as well as he had.

"So, are you bunking with me?" Storm asks with an eyebrow wiggle.

My cheeks burn a little at the thought, but I'll bite. Leaning into Storm's shoulder, I whisper, "I mean I sleep with this dagger, so that's really up to you. I can't guarantee you won't get a little poke if you get too close."

He gulps and stays silent. *Guess that's a no,* I laugh to myself. Although, if I'm honest, I'd hoped he'd say yes. The last few days have taken their toll and I'm aching for comfort. Groaning inwardly, I fold my arms. "Want to lead me to where the bunks are?"

Storm clears his throat. "Uh, sure. Right this way."

Below deck isn't as fancy as Wendell's cabin, but it's a hell of a lot better than the cell. There's rows of hammocks and a few bunks in the crew's quarters which gets me wondering.

"Where's everyone else? There's no way Wendell manages this ship alone," I turn in a circle.

"In that ye be right, lass," Wendell appears as if out of nowhere. "Me crew brought in about four coffers of booty just this morning, so they be out celebrating with a few wenches, if you know what I mean," he winks. "I don't expect they'll be back for a few days."

"Oh," I bite my lip.

"Have you chosen a bunk?" Wendell wraps an arm

around my shoulder. "Or would ye rather take yourself up to my quarters, it's a lot less ... drab."

My spine tingles at his closeness. Our eyes meet and something not yet clear passes between us. Throwing caution to the wind, I put an arm around his waist and gesture for him to take the lead.

"Hey!" Storm calls from behind us. "That's not fair!"

"Aye, all is fair in love and war," Wendell laughs over his shoulder as we climb the stairs.

The small trip from the crew's quarters to the captain's seems miles longer with Wendell's arm around me. It's nice having such close contact after the stress I've had lately. Deciding not to overthink it, I relax into it.

"Here we are," Wendell closes the door behind us and points to the large bed tucked into the corner. "It's about as luxurious as ye can get on a ship. I pride myself on me quarters," he beams.

"I bet you do," I step out of his hold and take in the space. There are fancy silks and rugs all about, and not a few trinkets. More or less what I'd expect, I guess. Walking over to the bed, I sit on the edge and sink into the fluffy mattress. "Oooh!" I laugh and lay back.

"Aye. 'tis nice, eh?" Wendell plops down beside me.

Turning to face him, my smile fades and I bite my lip. A pulse of static fills the air between us and before I can take a breath, Wendell grabs my chin and plants his lips on mine. His lips are firm and know what they're about as they seek entrance to my own. A deep well of need pulls at my core and I give in, opening my mouth to his. Our tongues tangle and Wendell reaches his other hand up my blouse, knocking my shell to the side with ease. My nipples peak and I let out a little moan of sadness when his lips leave mine.

"So, it is true what they say about the ladies of the sea." Wendell snickers as he lets the shells drop to the floor. His eyes meet mine with a question as he leans over me.

"Yes," I breathe as I pull him toward me, not knowing which question I'm answering.

Wendell lets out a shiver before his lips seal over mine again. The kiss melts me and sets me afire all at once. I realize I need more, so much more to drown out the hurt deep within. I don't want to be anything but a horny woman in front of a sexy man. "Please," I plead, hoping he will eclipse it all if even for a moment.

"It would be my pleasure," Wendell dips his face into the well of my breasts, licking and kissing his way to my neck. Waves of pleasure roll through me and I grab at his shirt, wanting naked flesh against my own.

Wendell sits up, pulling off his shirt and revealing his taut muscles. A kraken tattoo wraps around his ribs, the tentacles reaching down toward his nether region. One I realize I'd like very much to see. Scrambling out of my skirt, I keep my eyes fixed on Wendell. His breath catches as I lean back against the pillows, legs open.

"Blimey, you are beautiful. Dangerous, aye, but beautiful all the same." He undoes his trousers and pushes them downward freeing his manhood.

No matter the price, I want him. Wrapping my legs about his waist, I urge him forward. With the grace of a tidal wave, Wendell mounts me. He drives his long shaft into me hard, biting my chin at the same time. Lifting my hips, I urge him on. Every thrust of his hips sends me higher and further away from the pain. My muscles clench and I wrap my legs around him needing more.

"Tell me, lass," Wendell licks my earlobe. "How hard do ye need it?"

"As hard as you can give," I growl. His chest rumbles in response and he brings my legs up over his shoulders. Watching his beautiful landscape of planes, tight abs, and dark eyes sends me plummeting off the cliff.

"Aye, come me, little beauty." Wendell slows his thrusts, his focus totally on me.

With his eyes ravaging me, I come apart. Throwing back my head, I let the waves of ecstasy wash over me until I feel I'm drowning. Fire rages through my veins and I labor to breathe as Wendell lets go of my legs and leans forward. His lips trace along my jaw and he pushes deeper into my core, prolonging the pleasure.

Melting within his hold, I catch a glimpse of Wendell's face. His sinewy arms hold me captive as his pace quickens. The tight line of his lips loosens into an o and he moans deliciously. Captivated by the primal look on his face, I find my body responding to him with another small orgasm. Depleted, he collapses, turning us both on our sides. Sated and exhausted, I cuddle into his hold and close my eyes.

WENDELL

The ship's gentle rock had lulled me to sleep. Waking with the princess wrapped around me is a treat I hadn't planned. Her porcelain skin and long, red hair are unmatched in any I've had in bed before.

"Aye, little lass, wake up?" I whisper into her ear. Hopefully, we've woken before Storm so that she may decide how to proceed with our dalliance.

Her beautiful blue eyes spear me as they flutter open. "Do I have to?" She yawns.

"I'm afraid so." I untangle myself and leave the bed reluctantly. "Let me look about and see if I can find ye some clean clothes."

It's not hard to find a pair of pants, top, and vest that will fit Ari. She slides them on without batting an eye, which stimmies me loins For the finale, she drapes a purple bandana over her gorgeous locks. Aye, a princess that's practical is a boon. It doesn't go unnoticed that she looks natural in me pirate gear.

Once we're both up and dressed, I head down to the crew deck. "Time to wake, Sleeping Beauty!" I laugh as I poke Storm in the shoulder. "We are heading to the blacksmith. Are you coming?"

He pops open an eye and grunts, which gets me giggling.

"Fine, Ari and I are off to see Oli. You can roll over or come along. The choice be up to ye," I say as I take a step back.

"It's too early to be up," he grumbles as he gets out of the bunk.

I kick a few of the empty bottles at the base of the bunk, "Why is all the rum gone?" I ask, knowing exactly what transpired in the crew deck. Sadly for Storm, me crew is out and about, so it was Storm alone getting three sheets to the wind.

"Well, I didn't have a beautiful woman in my bed with me, so rum it was," he replies with a grimace.

I can't blame the bloke. If Ari had stayed with him last night, I would've drowned my sorrows in the bottles as well. Instead, I had the time of my life with a Princess.

"Ye be coming or not? Ari and I be headed into town in the next few," I remind him once more before turning and leaving.

With a skip in my step, I head back up to a waiting Ari. In the rays of the sun, her features are more striking than they were last night. She is a true beauty without even trying.

"Why are you smirking?" she asks with her brow furrowed.

I didn't realize that I had been smiling. "Aye, it's just a wonderful day, is all. Storm will be up in a few and we be on our way shortly," I wave my hand in the air. "Make sure ye speak up, rub in that headache he be having. He drank all me rum." I clasp me heart as if in pain.

"That wasn't a bright thing to do," she comments as her eyes look past me. I turn my head just as Storm appears. His rumpled clothing and furrowed brow make a sad picture.

"Morning," he mumbles without looking up from the floor.

"SLEEP WELL?" Ari practically yells at him.

Storm places his hands on his temples and sighs, "Not so loud, please. Can either of you dim the sun?"

"I'm a princess, not a witch," Ari shrugs.

"Pirate," I reply, pointing at myself with a huge grin.

"No would have worked," Storm shakes his head. I can't help but laugh at his self-imposed pain.

"Aye, help me with the gangplank and we be on the way," I say, motioning to the wooden ramp he helped me move last night.

"What would you do without me?" His face brightens a wee bit.

"Just use the rope," I shrug, "but this be for the Princess. Unless she fancies hanging along the edge, then the plank it be."

"I'd rather not," Ari comments.

Storm walks over and manhandles the gangplank and drops it into place with a grunt. "Your highness," he states with a little bow.

"Stop it, someone will hear you. What happened to laying low?" she asks as she stomps by without looking at him.

"Aye, hurry up, Storm. If we are to beat the morning

rush, we must make haste. Less eyes on Ari," I state as I follow Ari.

He mutters something but speeds up to keep pace with us.

Ari walks in between the two of us, eyeing the town in the daylight. It's as if I be seeing it for the first time as I watch the wonder light up her blue orbs. Her fingers flutter near mine, brushing against mine from time to time but never grabbing hold.

Storm is playing the strong, silent type, so I do what I do best. Talk. Just to annoy him, mostly.

"So, do ye have any idea where we be starting to find those that did this to ya?" I take Ari's hand and tuck it in me elbow.

"Well, I may have to sing to my little friend here and see if she has a lead for us," Ari pats the satchel I had given her the day before.

"'No' would've been an easy reply," I say, bumping my shoulder into hers.

"And what fun would that be?" she asks with an eyebrow raise. Her spunk does something to me insides, so I look up to gather me wits.

"Aye, we are almost to Oli's, let me do all the talking. He is a quiet man and I don't think I've ever seen him chatting with a woman," I tell the lot of them.

"So, he doesn't like women?" Ari asks with a smirk returning to her lips.

"I didn't say that, just a little shy, I think." I don't think my words are wrong, but it's not something that we ever talked about, Oli and I.

"I'll be on my best behavior," she promises, before

turning to Storm. "Could you do me a favor while we meet with the blacksmith?"

"Aye," Storm mutters, still not looking either of us in the eye.

"Could you run to the inn and check on my little, red friend? I may have to retrieve him and set him back into the ocean. I hate that, because he has the habit of running to my father and tattling on me. But I want to make sure he is okay," she says in a rush.

"Got it, make sure the crab is okay. Do not free him or eat him. No problem." Storm chuckles at his own joke.

Ari herself looks a little taken aback at his words. "Eat him?"

"Never, love. It was a joke. I'll check on him, I'm sure he is fine," Storm tries to make a serious face but fails, smiling instead.

It is nice that his mood seems to be improving, maybe he just isn't a morning person, but then again, I wouldn't be, either, if I drank as he had. I set my hand at my hip, enjoying watching the exchange.

"Okay, then go and meet us back here." Ari motions for him to get moving.

Storm gives me a little nod before he heads off back to the inn. Ari watches him leave, her lips pursed.

I wait a beat before questioning Ari. "You had a crab in your satchel.I'm How did that happen?"

It was Ari's turn to smile. "It's just part of who I am. You haven't heard the tales?"

It's true enough I took off her shell under...thing just last night, but I figured that was for shock value. I was still sure the tale of Prince Eric's wife, a mermaid that made a deal with a sea witch for legs, was too fantastical. That couldn't truly be this beauty's story, could it? Mermaids are things of legends and myths. Not one pirate I know has come face to face with a creature like that.

"Aye, but it's not one that I've believed in. You know how people are once they've had a nipperkin or two." I mime downing a bottle.

She starts to say something, but I interrupt as we have made it to Oli's shop.

"And here we be, Ari," I announce as we step up to a stone building with its two double doors wide open. Oli is already hard at work, striking the hammer onto heated metal. The heated iron and steel smell like earth and fire rolled into one, it's unmistakable.

"Oy, Oli. Got a minute for a friend?" I call between hammer strikes.

He stops his work and glances up at me with a soot-smeared face. A smile tips his lips, that is until he notices who is standing next to me. Oli's expression turns grim as he sets down his hammer and makes his way toward us.

"Aye, what can I do for you Wendell?" he asks, eyes bouncing back and forth from me and Ari.

"My friend, here, has a dagger that needs some care and a proper case. I told her that you'd be the chap to get her squared away," I explain with a smile.

Oli's eyes brighten at my words. "May I see the dagger?" he asks, holding a palm out toward Ari.

Ari fists the satchel with hesitation. "Yes, but I

refuse to leave it here. It's a family heirloom and I can't bear for it to be out of my sight. It's the one thing I have left of them." She purses her lips.

"Understandable, I promise to handle her with care." Oli motions again with an open palm.

Reluctantly, Ari hands over the weapon. I daresay Oli's eyes almost pop out of his head as he takes a wee gander at the piece. "My, she's a beaut," Oli whispers.

Oli brings the blade into the light, inspecting it from tip to hilt. He mumbles a bit to himself as Ari and I watch expectantly. She seems to lean toward the dagger as if it has a hold on her, which since it be magic —no doubt about that crosses me mind.

"T'will be my pleasure to work on this dagger for you." Oli turns to Ari. "It's well made, I can see why you don't want to have it out of your sight. I'll just sharpen and oil the blade, then I'll see which of the scabbards I have fit it best." Oli walks toward his tools.

If I'm not mistaken, the ruby at the hilt glows faintly as he holds it. Looking over to Ari, I wonder if she noticed it, too. I can't help but think that the glow means something. Scratching the few hairs on my chin, I lean against the wall as I mull the events of last night over in me head.

"Are you good with a sword?" Ari steps closer to Oli as he oils her blade.

He eyes her for a long minute before looking up from the dagger with a worried expression. "It kind of comes with the territory." He gestures to the shop. "Why do you ask?"

Ari fidgets, something I have yet to see her do. Any

fast thinking pirate would recognize she's collecting a circle of trust to aid her in her quest. Interested to see where this is going, I fold my arms and watch.

"It's hard to explain, but Harmony is signaling to me that you should be trusted." Ari points to the ruby.

Oli holds the dagger up to the light and the ruby flashes three times. A chill runs down my spine and I move closer. "Aye, don't be tricky, lass," I warn, remembering how I was inducted.

Ari scowls at me, "I'm not being tricky!" She places a hand on Oli's shoulder. "The blade is magic, I need your help in my quest but you'll have to swear by the dagger before I can tell you any more," Ari's voice drops to an intimate whisper. "Please?"

Oli looks to me for reassurance and I give him a nod, hoping I'm doing right by me matey. It's hard not to get caught up in the lass's eyes, throw in a magical dagger and none of us buckos have a chance.

A determined look falls over Oli's face as he turns to the princess. "Okay, I'll swear."

ARI

Swearing Oli in takes less time than the other two men, I've gotten a rhythm by now. It takes a little longer to appraise him of my situation, but weirdly, he accepted my story a little easier than Wendell. I've got a feeling Harmony spoke to him when he was fixing her up.

It didn't hurt that he was easy on the eyes and worked shirtless. The soot that was smeared on his face and body accented his features more. He even had a slight resemblance to my Eric, at least the hair and eye color.

With Oliver now part of the crew, a completeness settles in my bones. I've been hesitant to use Harmony until now but I think she's ready. At least I hope she's done collecting men to aid me, otherwise I'm going to have a hard time keeping a low profile.

"It is enough," Harmony whispers as if on cue.

"Here's two scabbards you can pick from," Oli's voice startles me as he exits the back room where he stores his leather goods.

"I'll take the red one," I answer without even

looking at the second one. Oli smiles conspiratorially before handing it over. The leather fits perfectly over Harmony's blade. It takes a moment for me to slide the scabbard onto the belt Wendell gave to me, but once it's done I let out a sigh of relief.

"Aye, that's a perfect fit for you, lass." Wendell steps to my side, eyes sparkling. The slight lift to his lip makes me tremble a little inside. He's suave without trying; really, it should be a crime.

"So, what'd I miss?" Storm walks in, looking from me to Wendell.

"The greedy dagger recruited Oli to our side," Wendell points to my hip. "Seems a fair group ye got, what's the plan now?"

Storm's mouth opens in astonishment, but I hold up a hand to quiet him before he begins. "I know this is a lot. It is for me, too. Now that we're all together, I think it's time to activate Harmony and begin our pursuit in earnest. Oli, can you get the guys proper weapons? This mission will not be bloodless," I grit. "I've vowed not to leave any that were involved in Eric's demise standing. Then there's also the Goddess's vengeance that will have to be attended to as well," I add as an afterthought.

"Right. Come with me, fellas," Oli replies without hesitation. My heart does a little somersault as I watch the three of them walk toward a wall of weaponry. I was warned that I'd be changed by the dagger, but I didn't factor this new relationship dynamic into the oath. Whatever Moryana has up her sleeve, I hope it doesn't end with me having to say goodbye to these three.

"They're mine now." I grab Harmony's hilt.

"Yessss," she replies, warming at my touch. *"Yours to keep. It is time for vengeance."*

Without thought, I begin humming a tune so familiar to me, it's a part of my soul. Only, this time, the notes seem darker, heavier somehow. A red glow fills the room and the guys turn toward me, eyes wide.

In the fire an image appears. It's a large cottage by the sea. The image wavers for a moment, then shifts until three women come into view. Their lips are moving, but there's no sound to the projection. I'm confused until one of them holds up a whistle. It's the same one that belonged to my lost love. A heat burns in my chest as she cradles the instrument in her hand. Then the image dissipates, leaving me breathless.

"Any of you recognize that cottage, or those women?" I look at my men.

"Aye, lass, I know the place," Wendell steps forward.

"And I recognize one of the ladies," Oliver gulps. "She purchased three swords from me not four days past."

"Is that normal? For a Princess to buy multiple swords?" I ask with tight lips.

"Aye, the patrons that come and see me aren't usually on the up and up. I have to make coin somehow, and these days, you can't be too picky," he replies honestly.

"That may be true, but I just had to check. Did you

count how many guards that trailed her?" I ask hopefully.

He shakes his head no. "'Tis not what I do when I'm helping a customer."

"Well we need to scout the cottage and plan our attack. We can't just go in blind," I say as a stomach rumbles from my left. I turn towards Storm with an eyebrow raised. "Are you trying to tell me that you have other ideas?"

This gets the three to laugh.

"What if we stop and grab a bite before we scout the cottage? It be hard to sneak up on anyone with noisy stomachs and all."

"Fine, lead the way. But conceal your weapons, don't want to be spooking any of the villagers with you lot," I state before asking Oli, "Do you need any help closing up shop?"

"Nah, I have a lock for the armory but the rest won't be touched," he says with a wide smile.

This piques my interest.

"Aye, the last person to steal from me, let's just say they have a beautiful ocean view with the anchor I fashioned for their ankle."

"A man after my little cold-current heart," I smirk.

Oli leads us out of the little room and locks the doors behind us. He gives the chain a tug and makes sure that the lock is tight. He nods and Wendell leads us back to the street as we travel toward the sea. The water calls to me, almost whispering for me to jump in. A shiver runs through me at the thought. I will not swim away from my problems. I promised vengeance, and I will have it.

"Ari, are you listening?" Storm asks, shaking me from my thoughts.

"What? Yes, sorry," I reply.

"I was saying there is a little galley near the sea. It will be the perfect place to grab some grub so we can form a plan. Will that work for you?" he asks.

"Yes, that's great for me," I lie with a smile. What am I going to enjoy at a seaside cafe? I still can't stomach eating fish and have avoided seafood altogether since I gave up my fin.

Wendell slows his steps to walk next to me. I guess after last night, he thinks that he knows me better than the other two.

"Are you sure about the galley? There will not be much other than seafood there. What will you eat?" he asks.

"Are you reading my mind? I'll be fine. Food is the last thing on my mind at the moment. Revenge will sate my thirst," I say with a smile.

"Aye," is all he says but the thought behind his check-in does something to my insides. Two days ago, I was alone in the world, and now—this. Rather than try and sort my feelings, I think of conversation.

"Storm, did you leave Sebastian any water? Or will we need to check on him again soon?" I ask, raising my voice so he can hear me.

"That I did, he wasn't too excited to see me. He attached his claw to my nose and I had to pry him off," he remarks.

I can't contain the laugh that escapes my lips. "If he wouldn't run off to my father, I would free him."

"Why would he do that?" Oli asks. "And... just so I'm clear, we are talking about King Triton, right?

"Yes, my father, a demigod, is the king of the sea. As for Sebastian, it's just what he does. The little crab thinks he's helping, but most of the time he accidentally makes things worse. His heart is in the right place but sometimes, you have to make your own mistakes to learn from them." I blow a stray strand of hair from my eyes.

"Aye, that is the best option. The hotel is paid up for a few days, he'll be okay there. Stella will leave your stuff be, I had a little chat with her when I checked on your friend. Just told her you have some business around the coast but you would pay for every night until we checked out. As long as she gets the coin she doesn't care if you stay there or not," Storm states.

"That was kind of you to do so. Thank you," I touch his arm. It eases my mind that he will be safe where he is and not on someone's plate. Storm slows his pace as a little shack comes into view, but the waves rolling into the shore are what have caught my eye.

"Do ye miss it?" Wendell asks.

"Yes and no. I don't have the time for nostalgia now. Harmony demands blood and I will comply," I reply honestly.

"Right, vengeance now. Got it, but food first," Storm pipes in as he leads us to a free table. The eatery is little more than a dockside shanty with a dozen or so tables and a long bar adorned in fishing nets. A chill runs down my spine as I look up to see a huge stuffed marlin. I should be used to such sights, but they catch me off-guard each time.

A bar maid sets down four drinks in the middle of the table, startling me. "What'll it be?"

"Three specials and one salad dish," Storm answers without hesitation. I glance over to him and smile. Unbeknownst to me, these men have already started picking up on the things I like and dislike.

"Whatever you say, cutie," she winks as she heads back towards the kitchen. I swear if I had a coin for every woman who batted her eyes at Storm, I'd have a pocketful already. Determined to get myself together, I fold my hands in my lap.

"So, how far is it to the cottage?" I ask, trying to get us back on track.

"Maybe a mile or so," Storm states.

"Is there any way we can sneak up on them? I think that a surprise attack will be our best bet," I say as I brave a sip of my drink.

It burns as it goes down and a little cough escapes my lips. The three men smirk at me before raising their glasses and emptying them all at once.

"Why didn't you warn me that the drink would burn? I slap the table.

"It's a trial by fire here. They will chuck us out if we tattle," Wendell explains. "I'll give ye a little hint for the future, if it comes in a short glass—t'will burn."

Storing the information for later, I lean back in my seat. I haven't fully thought my mission through. Am I resolved enough to actually kill a person? Coldness washes over me. As I press deeper into my mind, I'm certain that I can.

"Earth to Ari." Oli waves his hand in my face. His blue eyes strike a cord, bringing back memories of Eric that I'd rather not face at the moment. I gulp back the grief that could easily overwhelm me had I not ventured out on the task at hand.

"Yes?" I find myself agitated at my lack of presence lately.

"You should eat," Oli motions to the salad in front of me as he ladles a spoonful of chowder in his mouth. I'm relieved to see there's no chunks of fish on anyone's plate. Chowder is something I could eat as well, I realize as my stomach lets out a yowl.

"Can I try?" I reach for his utensil. Oli smiles wide, then pops the spoonful into my mouth. The creamy warmth settles on the back of my tongue and I swallow with relish. Something warm in my belly is definitely on the menu. Without thinking, I grab the piece of metal and take a few more bites. Before I know it, the bowl is empty. Sitting back in my chair, I take a deep breath.

"Aye, a lass that can eat, me like," Wendell winks as he pushes my bowl toward Oli.

The rest of us laugh as Oli shovels down my salad quickly. There's a camaraderie forming, although I'd bet the men already being familiar has helped, which is comforting. In my lifetime, I've only had a few close friends.

"Shall we be off then?" Storm rises. "I think I know just the place we can sit and wait for nightfall."

SINGING DAGGER

"Yes, that's perfect. Someone pay the tab?" I look around for the ladies' room and head in the direction of the door with a female over it. One thing about being a land dweller I'll never get used to is having to relieve oneself over these contraptions that spit water and yowl in return. As quickly as I can, I get the whole dirty business done and wash up before joining the men.

"Everything come out all right?" Oli chuckles.

Sure that he's being silly, I scrunch my nose and put my hand into the crook of Storm's arm. "Lead on," I state.

Storm raises an eyebrow, patting my hand with a smirk to the other men. I've not had a lot of practice with humans, but mermen are just as cheesy when they get the female. Shaking my head, I point forward, hoping to get us back on track.

The walk from the galley to the shoreline is quiet. Most people seem to have eaten lunch and retired for a nap if the couple resting in hammocks on their porches is any indication. Relieved not to have eyes on me, I take in a lungful of air.

"Are you taking us to the cave on the beach?" Oli asks.

"Yep, the same one we used to practice our sword fighting when we were wee lads," Storm smiles. Its position will allow us to sight the cottage as the sun sets. I figure we can scale the cliff beside it once darkness covers."

"Good thinking. It wouldn't hurt for us to have a

round of practice as well." Wendell pulls out a snarf-blatt and lights it.

"Right you are," Oli agrees.

With that settled, we make our way to the end of the lane. A winding trail takes us down to the beach. A few paces later, we rounded a bend to see the cavern. Across the water, a large, white cottage rests against the cliff. There's a white fence around the side, but a perfect view into the window that faces the sea.

"Let's get to work then, shall we?" I walk into the cave and unsheathe Harmony.

ARI

Turns out the whoosh of the tide coming in is the perfect cover for our practice. Blades clash together as Oli and Wendell have a round with no one the wiser up top. The two men have shed their shirts in a display of muscled magnificence. If we weren't headed on a murderous quest come dusk, I'd try for a little more nudity.

"Are you sure this is the only way to clear your name, princess?" Storm squats at my side.

Turning to face him, I draw my brows together. "Do you think anyone in Tirulia would take my side?"

The tracker shakes his head. "No, I suppose not. Things might be different if you weren't a foreigner, not to mention the stuff of legends. There's so many shepherd tales running around now I bet," he sighs.

"Humans aren't very kind to one another, much less someone like me," I whisper as I watch the last rays of the sun disappear. "It's time. Gather the men and let's go."

Storm lets out a whistle which stops the fight. Both men are quick to gather themselves and step to my side. Gripping Harmony tight, I begin to hum. The dagger warms before it tugs me in the direction of the cottage. With the men behind me, we follow the beach along the edge of the water until we reach the cliff underneath the cottage. A small yacht is docked at the edge, which I note for later.

"If there's a boat here, they must have stairs," Oli walks around the dock. "Here! Let's go!"

"Aye, don't be foolish enough to use the stairs. Crouch beside them and make yer way up to the top under the cover of the reeds," Wendell slaps Oli in the back of the head. If we weren't on a dangerous mission, I'd sit and laugh. As it is, I muffle my mouth with a hand and pass the men to begin the trek upward.

My calves burn by the time the fence comes into sight. The three of us lean our backs against the wood as we catch our breath. Voices murmur from behind the window and I turn to see who it might be. Sitting at a table are three blond-haired women. Behind them, I spot at least three men stationed against the walls.

"I'm telling you Quinn, we need more men!" one of the ladies shouts as she stands, knocking over her chair.

"'Tis the one that bought the swords," Oli whispers near my ear. His hot breath fans my neck, sending a shiver down my spine. *Stop it, Ari, focus on the mission.*

"How has she managed to evade both us and the royal guards? That flaming redhead is a beacon," another states.

"We be listening to them flap their jaws all night or we fight?" Wendell asks from my right.

"Let's wait until a guard exits and we can surprise them," Storm pipes in.

"Great plan, now less talking," I say, a little annoyed. What part of 'watch and attack' does this trio not understand?

"Blood," Harmony hisses.

I pat the sheath, hoping to quiet her until I can give her what she wants. As if on cue, the front door slams open, creaking on the hinges as two figures exit.

"Now," I whisper and all three men move at once like a great wave. Storm takes down the first one in a matter of seconds. The second guard proves to be a little more handy with a blade. Wendell is holding his own as the other guard arrives. Oli doesn't hesitate and jumps in the fight, leaving me free to enter the cottage.

The three women jump up from where they were seated at the dining table.

"Who are you and why are you in here?" the closest one to me asks.

I hold Harmony up, flashing the blade in the candlelight, "I'll be asking the questions. Now sit."

None of them move.

"I SAID SIT!" I wail with such force that the walls shake.

All three of them scramble to find a seat, almost knocking each other over in the process. The scene draws a thin smile to my lips even as my blood boils at the thought of their treachery.

"Is there any rope in this little shack?" I ask, kicking myself for not provisioning for such an occurrence.

No reply, so I move toward the closest one and

press the blade to her neck. "Answer me, or I will spill your blood."

She gulps, "In the next room. The guards had some in there that they were supposed to use."

"Storm," I call, not moving the blade from where I hold it.

Storm enters, wiping blood from his blade onto his pant leg, "You rang, Ari?"

"Will you grab the rope in the other room? I say we tie them to the chairs so there won't be any trying to run off as we have a chat."

"Aye," is all he says before he disappears into the next room.

Wendell makes an appearance just in time to tie up the princesses. I stand guard with Harmony still in view in case they get any ideas of escaping.

"Usually, women are asking me to tie them up," Wendell jokes as he finishes his task.

"Did you take care of the guards?" I question as I ignore Wendell's statement.

"Aye, one got away but Oli is chasing after him. Won't be long until he be back," Wendell assures me.

"Can you loosen these things?" one of the princesses whines.

Disregarding her question, I start with my own once again. "Who sent you?"

Silence.

"Why did you kill my husband?"

Nothing.

"I'll make them speak," Harmony whispers.

"These ropes are too tight," another one whines.

"Aye, you may not have noticed, but your comfort is none of my concern. Harmony, here, can remove that hand for ya or one of my men can manage with one of their swords," I bite out.

All three gasp.

"I have never," they all state at once.

"What are you three doing in our town? More importantly, why did you kill my husband?"

"Look, you crazy bitch, we don't even know who you or your husband are," the one called Quinn sneers.

Doubting their story, I grab the scarf from my hair and shake it out dramatically. There's a moment of silence before they all hiss, "It's you!"

"Surprise! Now answer me! Why were you looking for me? Who sent you?" I question again.

"I was told that you stole Eric from me," the curly blonde pipes in.

The other two quickly disagree. There's some statements from each claiming Eric as their own through some paltry meeting or another before I came along. Their chattering is loud and annoying. They even try to get at each other but one of them falls over flat on her face and I can't help but laugh.

I look down at her laughing "What did that solve? Other than you making an idiot of yourself?" Disgusted, I look at Wendell. "Sit her back up." I order, crossing my arms across my chest.

He gives me a little nod and complies with a pep in his step. The princess whispers a thank you as her tears still run free. Her slight once over of Wendell sends me into a fit of rage.

"Save the tears, we haven't even started the torture yet," I growl.

"Why are you doing this?" Quinn asks with a sob.

"You brought this on yourselves. I will get to the bottom of who killed my husband. My blade, here, guides me to those that are guilty and Harmony, here, says you three must die," I say through gritted teeth. My mouth almost waters at the thought of seeing each of these women squirm.

As I finish speaking, Oli returns, a little winded.

"Were you successful?" I ask, not taking my eyes off the women.

"Aye, dead men tell no tales," Oli replies to my utter delight. I rub my thumb along Harmony's cross guard as a thank you for bringing me these men.

"Hear that, princesses? Who's first? One way or another you will tell me who sent you," I promise.

"What are you going to do with us?"

"Blood," Harmony demands and my heart thumps a little harder. Raising Harmony in the air, I stalk toward the one named Quinn. I wrap my legs over hers and take a seat on her lap. "Looks like you're up first. Are you ready to talk?" I whisper as I drag the blade along her chin.

"You're going to kill us either way, aren't you? Why should we say anything?" she questions.

"Why, to clear your conscience, of course. But it makes no difference to me if you burn in what humans call Hell," I shrug as I skim Harmony down her neck. I don't apply any pressure, this is just to scare her.

She remains tight-lipped. "Fine, have it your way," I sigh before I begin to hum.

This time, Harmony sinks into Quinn's neck. A thin line of blood appears and she starts to gasp for air as the blood begins to run more freely. The shock and awe on her face brings heat to my cheeks. Harmony pulses in my grip, warming.

"More," the blade commands.

"T...Tw...Twins," Quinn finally spits out before she struggles to breathe more.

She gave me a clue, so I give her mercy of a sort. Without drawing out my pleasure, I plunge Harmony into her chest. The princess slumps over, freed from her fight.

"Which one of you is next?" I ask with a grin. The room is silent as I stand, then use Quinn's dress to clean my dagger.

"I'll tell you everything I know," the one that fell on her face cries. "Please don't hurt me. Quinn begged me to join her. I swear I tried to refuse!" The tears dropping off her cheeks do nothing for me.

"Lass?" Wendell holds his palms up in a question that I didn't expect. "You don't have to do this alone."

I look him over, chancing a glance to both Oli and Storm who've taken up positions behind the remaining women. I can tell by the gleam in their eyes, that they won't hesitate to take the blood for me—but this promise was mine and I will deliver.

"Your dedication doesn't go unnoticed and will be rewarded. I swore vengeance and it is I who must complete the task," I nod toward the remaining two.

Walking over to the nearest, I tip her chin toward me with the blade. "Tell me what I want to know."

Her hot breath fans my face as she exhales, "It all started with the twins. I don't know them personally, but I did meet them before we left. They each have a yellow eye. I remember feeling so strange when they stood as one had the left eye and the other the right, so that when they stood together, both lined up eerily. The opposite of each other. I thought it was really weird but I knew better than to question them about it."

"Kill her," Harmony states and I comply with one swift jab into the woman's chest. Her face falls and she becomes silent.

"Oh, last little song bird. Are you ready to sing ?" Wendell perches next to the last princess as I clean Harmony. Oli steps to my side, brushes a strand of hair from my face and walks with me across the room.

"They smelled of seawater," the woman's mouth turns in an o as I plunge Harmony deep into her chest. I've heard enough.

I stand and turn to my men, "I have an idea of who is responsible for the murder."

Oli bends to check the pulse of the last kill. Storm surveys the room with a wrinkle to his brow. The mess will have to be cleaned, for sure. I sigh, waiting for a response.

Wendell picks up my chin with a finger "Aye, lass. Do tell how you know the perpetrator with so little information." His mouth is so close to mine, it scrambles my brain for a moment.

Stepping back to clear my head, I sheath Harmony. "My greatest enemy was slain before I wed Eric, the sea witch. But I never accounted for her familiars. The two slimy twins must have taken human form somehow to get to me. It is the only explanation. The yellow eyes can't be mistaken, nor ordinary."

"I'm sorry, Ari, I'm not following you," Oli leans against the wall. "Slimy twins? Sea Witch?"

"I know I left some things out when I summarized my story for you. Not only was I a mermaid, but I was tricked by the sea witch into giving her my voice for a pair of legs. I thought that Eric would recognize me without it since I saved him during a storm. Anyway I was close to getting my voice back but the witch intervened and tricked Eric by disguising herself as a human with my voice. There was a huge fight at sea and Eric finally killed her with the mast of a ship. Anyway, to get to the twins—in all her years of terror, she had two familiars who helped her evil plots. I wasn't the first to succumb to her trickery. The two eels, Flotsam and Jetsam were her sidekicks. They found potential marks for her. No one thought to look for them after she was defeated. We all just assumed they went back to their old lives when her magic wore off, as did all the merfolk she imprisoned." I put my face in my hands.

"So? What now?" Storm asks. "How do we find them?"

Raising my face, I clench my hands. "First, we check the land. And then, we go to the sea."

ARI

Cleaning up the mess in the cottage takes more time than I'd have liked. We had to drag all the bodies down to the water and stow them on the boat before returning to clean up the blood. Never having killed anyone, I didn't know just how much of the red liquid would coat everything, especially me. It wasn't even a passing thought while I was killing, my intent was too pure. Now I wish I'd have at least tried to be a little neater.

"Now that the cleaning is done," I stalk over to Oli and pull him in for a long kiss. The tension built between us turns the small kiss into a volcanic eruption. Oli's hands roam down my back before cupping my asscheeks, pulling me flush with his body. A heat builds between us that's hard to deny, but deny it I must. Breaking the kiss, I turn to the others. "Let's dump the bodies in the sea and then find dinner—I'm starving."

Storm raises an eyebrow before he lets out a chuckle. "Who knew our fair princess would be so rough around the edges, eh?"

"What?" I shrug. "A girl's gotta eat, I just burned a lot of calories!"

The three men share a look before breaking out into smiles. Wendell chuckles, sweeping the last of the dirt out the back door. "Aye, I reckon we could all taste a wee bite of fare and enjoy a clap of thunder," he winks.

"I could certainly whet my whistle," Oli agrees.

"So, it's settled then," I clap. "Avast!" I giggle as I try pirate slang.

Going down the cliff is a lot easier on the muscles, that's for certain. Once we've boarded the boat, Wendell steps up to the wheelhouse. "Any particular dumping grounds you'd recommend, oh lady of the sea?"

Setting my hand on my hip, I scan the horizon to get my bearings. When that isn't enough, I lean over and dip my fingers into the water. A shiver runs down my spine and before I know it, I'm floating in the water, fin caught in my pants. Shimmying the cloth off, I gasp when I catch sight of my bottom half.

"It's black!" I shout as I surface.

Wendell looks around, confused. "Lass?"

"My fin! I raise it out of the water. It should be green, this is terrible!"

Oli peers over the side of the boat scratching his head. "I dunno, Ari, I think the black is quite stunning."

Frowning, I throw my pants at him, no use in crying over black scales. I conjure an image of the Goddess. She sure could have warned me, though.

"Come on, I'll lead you to where the shark sleeping

grounds are located. They'll be close to the surface about now, which makes for easy disposal of those bodies." I gesture out to the deeper part of the water from the cove.

Having not been in mermaid form for over a year, my body is a riot of sensations. I'd forgotten—or never appreciated—how freeing it is to swim. Splashing through the water, then diving deep and coming back again is invigorating. I'm enjoying myself so much, I hardly realize when we come to the deep ocean. The dark shape of a fin protruding from the water is a big wake-up call.

"Here we are." I surface. "Pull me in before I'm dinner."

Oli grabs one hand and Storm the other. In one fluid movement, they tug me out of the water and onto the deck. My fin hangs around just long enough for everyone to be staring when it disappears. Caught naked from the waist down, I bite my lip and grab for my pants.

"Quit gawking and throw the bodies over," I command even though I quite enjoy having these three sets of eyes on me at once. *For clam's sake, get it together, Ari.*

The bodies hit the water with a splash and fins come zooming toward the boat. Needing no direction from me, Wendell quickly gets the boat moving away from the feeding frenzy. Dressing quickly with semi-wet skin is totally ridiculous, but I manage to keep a little dignity about me.

"Shall we float to the next town over for our meal?"

Oli asks. "It would save us from worrying if Ari is spotted."

"Aye, that's a perfect idea, bucko," Wendell smiles. "We can dump the boat on their docks, too, and no one will be the wiser."

"Aye, the next town on the shore is a few miles, but if we take turns rowing we will be there before too long," Storm states as he takes the oars from Wendell.

"What is our next move?" Oli asks, not really looking me in the eye.

The things that I just did are nothing that I would have dreamed that I was capable of, but the Goddess did tell me that the blade would change me. I wouldn't shy away from it, nor be sorry for it. I was promised vengeance and I was willing to do what I had to.

"Oli," I say lightly, just to grab his attention. "Murdering people so easily isn't something I've always done. The Goddess changed me so that I might seek revenge. I should have realized the consequences of taking gifts from a deity, but I had no other options. Harmony is my blade of Vengeance and I will not apologize for that."

"As you shouldn't," he agrees. "Is it bad that it turned me on a little to watch you in control?"

This time, I smile. I think we will get along very well, Oli and I. The fear that was churning in my stomach settles and I take a deep breath.

"Mate, it wasn't just me then?" Wendell elbows Oli in a playful way.

I glance toward Storm and I can tell he is trying to

conceal the smirk on his lips as well. I was worrying for nothing, the blade chose my companions well.

"Aye, hand me the oars, Storm," I command as I settle in the middle of the little boat. "It's my turn."

"Nah, I'm good," he remarks as he continues to row.

"It's not a request. Hand them over," I state as I hold a hand toward him.

He sighs as he hands them to me. "Are you always this bossy?"

"You lot seem to have a thing for bossy women, why would I be any different?" I smile as I accept them.

Satisfied, I begin to row. The movement helps relieve some of the aggression that's been building ever since I was gifted the dagger. The Goddess told no lies, I feel less and less like the mermaid I used to be each hour that passes. Wendell starts to hum a familiar song.

"What song is that?" I ask.

In response, Wendell begins singing the words, "Yo ho, yo ho, a pirate's life for me."

I can't contain the smile that spreads on my lips. The little I know about these men is enough to burn them into my heart. It's not often you find people willing to kill for you. And yet, we're all here as if it's a normal day.

"Aye, is that the only song you know?" I ask with a laugh.

"Nay, but what better way to pass the time?" he questions before he starts up his tune again.

He repeats the verse a few times before he takes a turn with the oars. His voice is pleasant, even if the tune is silly. He stops abruptly, changing the tone of the ride from humorous to awkward in a matter of moments. The quiet is when what we just did settles deep in my bones, so when I spot the dim lights of the town we were searching for, I'm grateful.

"Aye, there be light," Oli calls. "We have reached Dead Man's Refuge."

"Huh, that's catchy," I comment without thought, "You humans have the strangest name for things."

"That may be, but I'm sure what merpeople name things are probably the same," Storm says, as he moves a little closer. He holds out a hand before asking, "Scarf? Maybe best to cover that beautiful red hair. There aren't many women with your shade and we don't want to be on the run. You never know how far the search for you has gone already."

"Smart thinking there, Tracker," I say with a smile and pull the scarf from my pocket before handing it over to him.

With care, he covers my locks and orders Wendell to tie it, since he is seated behind me. Once Wendell has it secure, Storm tucks a stray back in and runs a finger along my cheek.

I don't want him to stop but Oli calls out, "Land ho."

"What will we do with the boat?" I ask the three men.

"Fire," Storm says simply.

"'Fire?'" I parrot, but as a question.

"Aye, there is blood in the cracks of the boards. Fire be the only way to get rid of the mess," Wendell strokes his chin. "They be looking for the boat soon. This is the best action."

"Will it burn on the water? Or will we have to plug it on shore?" I ask.

"Best bet is to start a little blaze on shore and push it into the water. It will burn mostly before sinking," Wendell says.

We lurch forward as the bow hits the sand. I'm not prepared for it and I land in Storm's lap. My first instinct is to wrap my arms around his neck.

"Well, hello there." He smirks as he wraps his hands around my waist.

"Sorry," I say, flustered.

"I'm not, you should see Wendell's face right now," he whispers as he pulls me in a little closer.

I glance back and note a little jealousy has crossed the cheeky pirate's face. So, instead of jumping up, I stay where I am and cup Storm's face as I guide his lips to mine. I brush against his lightly but he wants more and places a hand on the back of my head to keep me close. His kisses are greedy and almost bruising, but I don't break away until he does.

"I've been waiting for that since you first walked into my cottage," he states a little out of breath.

"Well, what took you so long?" I grin as we stand to exit the little boat.

"I wasn't sure if you wanted me or not. But since you started the kiss, I wasn't going to let you get away so easily," he replies with a huge smile that lights up his eyes.

Wendell pipes up, "Ye want me to light the boat on fire with you two in it?"

There is a hint of annoyance in his tone, which I wasn't expecting.

"Jealousy isn't a good look on ye, Wendell," Storm says as he helps me from the dingy.

"Aye, I need a drink," is all he says in reply.

Oli, on the other hand, doesn't say anything at all. I look between the three of them, mouth pinched. A talk is in order, because I refuse to ping-pong around the fact that I'm drawn to all three. Peering down at Harmony on my hip, I frown, *"This is your doing."*

Harmony is quiet, but her ruby flares for a moment. Shaking my head, I walk toward the guys with Storm at my side. Wendell and Oli quickly gather a few sticks of driftwood. I watch as they create torches with the torn edge of Oli's shirt. Wendell produces a bottle of liquor. From there it's short work to start the boat on fire. We watch the flames consume the boards one by one before pushing it into the ocean.

"Let's get some grub. All this covering of our tracks has left me starving," Wendell comments as he takes off toward the little town.

"You aren't going to drink all the rum, are you?" I question.

"Aye, I just may."

"Well, remember we have to get back to the hotel so I can check on my little, red friend," I remind him.

"Fine, I'll be on my best behavior," he replies with a wink. My heart thumps at the easiness that returns between us. Letting out a chuckle, I slide my hand into his arm. I have a feeling that he could drink all three of us under the table and not bat an eye.

ARI

Turns out Dead Man's Refuge is little more than a hundred or so cottages surrounding a shoddy inn. My stomach growls as we walk from the beach to the lane. There's a few fishermen on their porches, mending nets as we pass. Most offer a slight wave, if they notice us. The town center is a well, which is abandoned at this time of night, and the inn.

"You sure we won't be fingered here?" I lean into Oli.

"Folks from the Refuge are here for a reason, Ari. They don't meddle in others' business. We will be just fine." He pats my shoulder. "With any luck, they'll have a room or two; walking to Tirulia from here would take the better part of the night."

Both hunger and apprehension bubble in the pit of my stomach, but I press forward, assured that my circle can handle anything that happens. The wooden sign, carved with a large dragon, swings in the wind. Storm steps out of the group to grab the door, holding it open as we step inside.

"Welcome to the Flaming Dragon!" a voice calls. "Find yer seats and I'll be over."

Oli leads us to a corner table near the grime-coated window. I take the seat nearest the glass while the guys eyeball each other, silently debating who will sit to my left. Oli grins widely as he plops down beside me. Taking a deep breath, I clasp Harmony's hilt to steady my heart.

"What can I do for you?" A stout man steps up to the table, wiping his hands on the white apron at his waist.

"Aye, is the kitchen still serving by chance?" Wendell asks. "We also be needing a might bit of rum and a room," his eye twinkles as he pulls out his coin purse and gives it a shake.

The barkeep eyes the purse with glee, nodding his head. "For paying customers, the kitchen and a room indeed!"

"Thanks, mate, we'll start with the rum and whatever you got that's warm," the pirate places a few coins on the table.

"You got it," the barkeep swipes the coin into one hand. "My name's Tyrus, holler if ye be needing anything more."

Within a few moments, a young girl appears with a tray of glasses. She sets them down with a shy smile before flitting away. Taking a glass in hand, I hold it in the air. "To our circle, may the company keep and the quest be fulfilled."

Glasses clink and I take a gulp of the fiery liquid. It burns, but settles the churn in my gut for which I'm grateful. We're two glasses in once Tyrus comes back with plates of stew. He sets them in front of us with a huge grin. "Me wife made this just today, and me boy caught the deer. 'Tis the best fare we have. The lass will have your room ready, just clap when yer ready."

He disappears before I can thank him properly, so I grab a spoon and dig in. The stew is perfectly spiced and flavorful. Delighted with the new meal, I quickly gobble it down. Setting my spoon on the table, I lean back in my chair and sigh.

"Is there anything you do that isn't fascinating?" Oli stares from my bowl to me. I shrug not understanding why eating is anything of note. The guys fall into quirks that they've noticed and I sit back, enjoying the camaraderie. It's unlike anything I've experienced. Looking out the window, I happen to overhear a conversation from behind us.

"Did you notice the two that have been lurking around lately? Weird sort, they are—give me the creeps."

When I turn my head, I see a buxom lady with an apron leaning over the table behind us. She and the fellow sitting are the ones conversing. By the apron, I can only guess that the lady is Tyrus's wife. Hoping to hear more, I signal the men to quiet.

"Aye, Bessie, you mean the guys with the double braids and yellow eyes?" The man raises his glass for the Bessie to fill. She nods, her lips set in a line, "Just the same. I hope they move on soon."

Wendell sets his glass down and leans toward Bessie,

"I'm sorry, M'lady, I couldn't help but overhear. Are the fellas a dangerous sort? What with us only in town for the night, we be wanting to avoid such," he smiles.

Bessie looks toward the corner with her eyes before she bends and whispers. "Tyrus don't like me meddling, but I've got a bad feeling about them, aye. Heard they was staying down by the docks. You and your lass will be safe here, my Tyrus runs an honest business." She nods emphatically before scurrying away as Tyrus calls her name.

The man left at the table tips his hat to us and we turn back in our seats. My throat dries as I think about Flotsam and Jetsam. I can't imagine what they might look like in human form, but the yellow eyes and double braids shouldn't be too difficult to spot. Harmony buzzes at my hip and I lick my lips. *"Soon."*

"Let's check into the room for a quick rest," Storm blinks his eyes as he looks me over. "They'll keep for a bit," he adds as if he knows I'd like nothing more than to go tearing off in search of the twins.

"Aye, we could all use a quick once over and rest before we set back out, let me see if I can rustle us up some clean clothing." Oli sniffs his underarm and frowns.

With that, we all stand and head over to the counter. Tyrus greets us with a smile before leaning over to grab a key from a row of nails behind him. "I see that yer ready to check in. It's room four up the stairs there. Anything else I can get ya?"

"Any chance you can find us suitable clothing? We

were marooned here when our friends took off without us. We'll pay extra," Oli offers.

"Let me see what I can do," Tyrus gives each of us a once-over as if recording our sizes in his head. "I'll send my girl, Elle, up with what I find. She's already drawn a bath in the room for you."

Happy to hear the last part, I snatch the key and rush up the stairs. Water always centers me and I can't wait to get out of these smelly garments. The key slides in the lock smoothly and I'm pleasantly surprised at the large room. There are two beds, a fireplace, and a wooden tub in front of the mantle with steam rising from it.

"This be a nice room," Wendell whistles. "I'll have to remember this place in the future."

"Do you want privacy while you bathe?" Storm holds the door open as if I'm going to kick them out.

"Why? I'm not ashamed of my body?" I walk over and shut the door. Without another word, I strip down and step into the inviting water. When I look back over my shoulder, all three men are standing with their mouths agape. With a laugh, I splash Oli, who's closer and lean back into the tub to relax.

"You three get comfortable and stop being weird," I call.

"Aye, easy for ye to say. Did you see the size of that bed? I didn't plan on snuggling so close to Storm or Oli," Wendell states as he slowly shakes his head.

"I'll be in the middle," I smile as I begin to lather up one arm, "makes no difference who lays next to me. Just a few hours of shut-eye is all I require."

"I will be back before you have finished your bath," Storm pipes in, "I have a few friends that should be up this hour. They may have seen who we seek, if they have, we can get eyes on them so we can form a plan of attack."

"That sounds promising," I state as I glance at him, noting the gleam of confidence in his eyes.

"I be joining him as well," Wendell sighs, "Fresh air may do me some good."

There are no more words spoken as the two of them head out. I haven't forgotten about the talk we need to have but this is the first time I allow myself to relax completely since my husband was murdered. It may be selfish but it's just what I need.

Oli clears his throat as if I forgot he is still in the room with me.

"Yes?" I raise a brow to him. His gaze is on the floor, which is quite cute.

"What do you need from me?" he asks, fidgeting with his fingers. I'd laugh, but I don't want to embarrass him more.

Sitting up, I turn toward him. "Look at me," I command, but my tone is light.

"As you wish M'lady," he says, rubbing the back of his neck before he musters the courage to meet my gaze.

"Are you normally this shy around a naked woman?" I smile slowly.

"What naked women? Most don't give me a second glance," he replies, as his eyes fall to the ground again.

"I don't believe that for one second. Strip," I command.

"Excuse me?" He returns his gaze to mine. The hesitance he has only makes me want him to obey more. A fire lights in my core and I purse my lips.

"I didn't stutter, strip and join me," I state as I pat the side of the tub.

"If that's what you wish," he says as he disrobes.

I watch every move he makes, he is a beautifully built man, chiseled like a god. Whomever these other women were, missed out royally. Drinking him in, I lift my knees to make space in front of me.

He slides into the tub, careful not to touch me, but I don't shy away. I lather up my hands and start to wash the soot from his arms. Oli tenses under my touch. It's almost as if he's forgotten the kiss we shared. Maybe he's less shy when clothes are involved. Amused, I pat him on the arm.

"Don't worry, I won't bite, unless you're into that?" I bite my lip to keep my smile from splitting my face in half.

My words finally get a smile from him. The way his eyes shine makes my heart beat rapidly. His courage doubles as he leans in close. Just as our lips would have met, there is a knock on our door.

"Yes?" I grumble.

A pretty, little, blonde woman pokes her head in as she apologizes, "Pardon me, M'lady. Wendell told me ye and your suitor, here, be needing some new clothes. I be setting them by the door."

"Thank you," Oli and I say in unison.

When the door closes behind her, Oli slips out of the bath.

"Leaving so soon?" I pout.

"It's for the best, you need some rest. I'll clean the weapons, can't have anything to trace back to us if the bodies are found," he says.

"Killjoy," I state with a smirk.

Oli grins sheepishly as he pulls on a pair of the pants. Folding my arms in protest, I frown. Oli surprises me when he doesn't replace his shirt. When he notices that I'm still watching him, he gives me a little wink.

Admitting defeat, I finish lathering myself. Oli rumbles around the room, searching the corners, looking for something.

"What are you doing?" I set down my rag.

"Trying to find a rag, my weapons won't clean themselves," he states as he holds a piece of cloth up in triumph. "Would you like me to clean your dagger as well?"

"That's a kind offer. Thank you. But can you show me the proper way so that I may care for her moving forward?"

"Aye, whenever you're ready, it will be my pleasure to teach you," he smiles.

"Are there any other things you can teach me?" I tease with a wink.

His cheeks flush and he doesn't answer, he just takes a seat and starts to work. I submerge myself for a few minutes, enjoying the peace and the water as it begins to chill. When I surface, Oli breathes a sigh of relief.

"M'lady if you were to stay in there any longer I would have come and pulled you out. Ye may have been a mermaid before, but I don't see a tail now. How is that?" Oli asks, glancing at the length of the tub.

"I've never thought much about it, I think it's because the water is boiled. It's not true sea water as I used to swim in," I reply in a light tone.

Oli goes back to cleaning when I decide that it's time to climb out and clean Harmony before getting some shut-eye.

"Oli?" I call his name and he looks up at me.

"Yes?" he questions.

"Will you help me up and hand me a towel?"

"Of course," he replies. As he stands, he grabs a towel before he holds a hand out for me to take.

Stepping into the towel, I grimace. A chill runs over my skin. Oli wraps the towel around me as soon as both my feet hit the dry floor.

"Thank you," I say breathlessly. Having him this close, I want him closer. Why the pull to all three of these men is so strong, I'm unsure, but I have a feeling that this is Harmony's doing. At least that's what I keep telling myself.

OLI

Being so close to Ari was torture. Sure, I've been near beautiful women before but she is different. There's a heightened pull to be close to her that I've never felt. It nearly drove me mad not to just throw her on the bed behind us and have my way with her. It's obvious that she's into me, as well as the other two and I don't know how to feel about it all. Between this deep need to be near her, and the thought of why she's pulled us together—I'm torn.

"Oli, I think that blade is clean enough." Ari plops beside me dressed in a thin gown, running a fork through her long locks.

Looking down at the cloth, it registers to me how long I've been lost in my lustful thoughts. There's a tenseness in the air, and I'm afraid I know the only way to relieve it. The question is—should I? Ari is beautiful and daring …. And dangerous. She's been through so much, can I trust her consent? What if she regrets being with me afterward? I couldn't bear it.

Turning toward Ari, I set the sword at my side. "How are you feeling?" I manage to stutter out.

Ari scrunches her nose, "Feeling about what?"

Raising my hands in the air, I let out a long breath, "This, everything. You've been through more trauma than most people have their whole lives in under a week!" Taking her hand in mine, I stare into her ocean-blue eyes and try for all that I have to see who she is underneath.

"I feel scared, angry, determined, and passionate," Ari leans in, lightly brushing her lips over mine. "The only reason I'm not falling apart right now is the three of you. Harmony brought you to me for a reason." She looks over to the dagger that's propped on a chair. "And I don't think it's just for the blood of my enemies."

"Do you … think of him?" I turn away. I can't imagine the hurt she must be hiding.

"Sometimes, but it feels so far away. I don't know how to explain it other than I think Harmony helps," she sighs.

"I understand your mission." I swallow. "My father and I hunted down the man who took my little sis from us," I choke out, remembering the night.

Ari freezes. Hoping I haven't said the wrong thing, I take her hand in mine. "There has to be more to this than killing them. Otherwise, you'll be left feeling hollow at the end." I stop before I lose control of my feelings.

"I know," Ari shifts her body toward me. "That's why I have you three. Let me in, Oli. I need you."

The door opens just as I dip my head toward Ari and I let out a groan.

"Sorry to, er, interrupt," Storm chuckles. "We found

nothing. Best we all rest for tonight." He sits on the other side of Ari. Wendell latches the door and begins pulling off his boots.

"You two better get in the bath before you even think of laying on this bed," Ari pinches her nose. "Did you visit the gutters while you were out?"

"Aye, the lass be trying to get us out of our clothing," Wendell jests.

Storm stands and crosses the room to stare into the now cold water. "Fetch the girl then, I ain't lathering in that."

With a fake sigh, Ari crosses the room and heads out the door. Amused, I make myself busy by putting the weapons away. There's something about looking at a freshly cleaned blade that satisfies me.

"I don't understand why you're still in your britches." Storm leans and sets his boots in front of the fire. "No way I'd have squandered time alone with Ari."

Shrugging, I step up to the window. "I'm not you. Have you two taken into account how much she's been through? You can't just jump her bones and not realize she just lost her husband!" I turn to face them.

They both manage to look sheepish and I shake my head. "So, what then? After you bed her?" By the wince, I can tell Wendell has already crossed that line. Rubbing my hand over my face, I sigh. "Please tell me you're planning to stick around after we've completed the quest."

Wendell throws back his shoulders, "Aye, what may you be implicating about my person? If the Lass will have me, I'll sail the world with her at my bow."

"What if she chooses me?" I open my palms.

"Or me?" Storm digs a thumb into his chest. "How do any of us know what Ari wants?"

At that, Wendell snickers. The door bangs open and Ari slams it behind her. "If you want to know what I want, the best way is to ask," she frowns. "I certainly don't need you trying to parcel me out to the highest bidder or the biggest dick!"

Her choice of language sends fire to my cheeks. "Ari." I sigh. "You have to at least acknowledge that we're all in a strange predicament. I think I'm speaking for all of us when I say there's an uncontrollable pull to you. You're the center of our small universe and we're just trying to see how we align."

Her face softens, but she stands firm. "This is my plight. Vengeance must be had, no matter the price. If you must know where you stand, you all stand at my side or leave now. I will not choose between the three of you, you are mine."

Storm steps toward her. "Yours for now? Or always?"

"Always must the circle be held," Harmony sings.

Frowning, I watch the ruby pulse with light. "Is magic the only reason we're together?"

"Nay, it has been written upon your souls," Harmony answers and her light flares.

The room falls silent. Not knowing what else to do, I turn back to the window. There's a knock on the door. The sound of it opening and closing seems far away as I search the stars. Water is poured and the door opens and closes again. My mind is racing, trying

SINGING DAGGER

to pick apart the events since I met Ari. I've never experienced magic and I'm not sure I'd have believed it had I not heard the dagger for myself.

There's a hand on my shoulder. "Come, lay with me while those two clean up," Ari whispers.

Taking one last look at the sky, I follow her to the bed. Stripping down to my underwear, I settle in next to her. She takes my arm and pulls it around her before closing her eyes. In seconds, her breathing changes and I relax next to her, knowing she's asleep.

I awake to the signs of first light, my internal clock has yet to let me sleep past this time of morning. Ari is still snuggling up next to me and I hate to get up, but if we are going to check the docks for these two that did this to her, now is the time.

With care, I shift her off my arm and onto Storm. Not sure when he joined us, but there's a smile on Ari's face when she settles her head on his chest. There is no jealousy as I gaze on them so content.

I stand and stretch before I eye Wendell snoring in the tub. I pull my pants back on as I make my way toward him, I hit the side of his boot that was hanging over.

"Oye," he protests as he opens one eye.

"Rise and shine, Sleeping Beauty," I say lightly and in a teasing tone.

Wendell glares at me as he holds his head, "Me thinks the rum won this round."

"The sun is starting to rise, if we want to slink around the dock, we need to leave now," I say as I step up to the window and glance out.

Just as I thought, there are little yellow and orange rays painting the sky.

"Aye," Wendell agrees as he takes a swig from a bottle I didn't see in the tub with him.

"You really think that's a good idea?" I ask, raising an eyebrow.

"Pirate, remember? Rum is the best cure for a hangover," he smirks as he scrambles to get out of the tub.

I hold a hand out and with a grimace he has two choices. Accept my help and drop the bottle or continue looking like an idiot and get out himself.

"Fine," he comments as he drops the bottle. He takes my hand after he carefully sets the bottle down.

It doesn't take much to get him to his feet, but to keep him standing is another story.

"Maybe you should stay here? We need to be stealthy and the way you are swaying, there is no way you're going to be as quiet as a pack of wolves," I comment.

"I be fine, now let's wake the others and get this going," Wendell comments with a hiccup.

Yes, this is going to go well. I cross back to the bed and give Ari and Storm a gentle shake.

"Wendell and I are heading to the dock, are you two going to join us?" I ask as I shake them again.

Storm tightens his hold on Ari but his eyes open and he gives me a little nod before he places a kiss on her forehead. Her eyes flutter open and she smiles at him before turning to do the same to Wendell and I.

Ari is the one to stretch and she has a calm demeanor since she's gotten some rest. "Let's get this show on the road. It's the first light, right? I could use a few more hours of shut-eye but I can get those later. Now is the time for tracking those twins."

"Aye," the three of us agree.

I take a seat on the bed to pull my boots on, then I stand to replace my sword belt on to my waist and I'm ready.

Storm and Ari pull on some of the new clothes that we were brought as well as their shoes, before she asks him to help cover her hair once again. It is a shame to cover those flaming locks but it is for the best. After ensuring there are no stray strands showing, we are ready.

Wendell eyes the amber bottle with longing but never moves to retrieve it.

"Which way to the wharf?" Ari asks as she heads to the door.

Storm beats her there and opens it for her. What a gentleman.

"I know the way, after you, M'Lady," he says with a weird, little curtsy.

Our steps are light, that is until Wendell falls down.

"Maybe it's best you stay here and sober up," I comment as I glance back at him.

"Oye, mind your own business, mate. I be fine," he says as he stumbles again.

"Your funeral when Ari stabs you for messing this up," I comment under my breath.

The owners are at the bar when the four of us make it down the stairs.

"The room not up to ye standards?" the wife asks.

"It was perfect, we just have a few errands to run this morning," Storm says as he places more coins on the counter.

"That's what we like to hear. No one will mess with your things. You are welcome to stay as long as needed." She smiles as she pockets the coins.

"Thank you," Ari says as we continue to the door.

Once we are out of the building, Ari asks, "Are people always this nice?"

"Aye, only when coin is involved, mostly," I tell her. "Here on land, gold and jewels will get you farther with people than if you don't have any. 'Tis the way of the world, sadly. Some work hard, day in and day out and never get ahead."

"Somedays, I wish I'd never discovered the human world, especially when I learn these things." She sighs.

"Are you going to sing to that dagger? Or are we going in blind?" Storm pipes up.

"Yes, it should show us where on the dock they are and if my suspicions are true," she replies.

The now familiar, almost haunted, tune fills our eyes and the dagger Ari holds starts to glow and spin on her palms.

It shows two men whispering to each other. There's no mistaking that they are twins, complete mirrors of each other. If they have the yellow eyes it's hard to tell

SINGING DAGGER

from what the dagger is showing. I take note that they are standing on a boat that is still tied to the docks and the name that is painted on the back confirms what Ari thought—SEA WITCH.

Their image fades as the dagger stops spinning and points in the direction of where there are a handful of ships.

"Let's pretend we are headed to a boat at the very end of the docks. Once we see where they are, we will make a plan from there," Ari says.

"Anything you say, Princess," I say when she turns and starts her walk.

ARI

A mix of excitement and trepidation fill me as we near the docks. In my experience, nothing ever goes as smoothly as planned. At least we have numbers on our side, four to two. The thing I'm worried about is magic. There's no other explanation for the twins being human. Who has been helping them with their little game?

The pier is one long strip with about ten boat slips. Stepping onto the platform, I stare at the names of each boat as we pass. Most of them are small fishing boats, but the one on the end looks like a pirate ship. Stopping to take it in, I let out a sigh of appreciation.

"Aye, don't go getting breathless over me rival," Wendell elbows me playfully then freezes with seriousness. "The Sea Witch is right next to her."

"We're too far to turn back now," I grimace as I unsheathe Harmony. "Let's go, boys."

Running toward the large sailboat, I scan for the two evil beings. My heart is thumping as we come up to the boat. A slight fog hangs in the air, making it hard to see from bow to stern. Without a thought, I climb over the rail and step onto the deck carefully. From the corner of my eye, I catch Wendell grabbing a rope and hoisting himself toward the bow. With Oli and Storm at my back, I tiptoe toward the cockpit.

"Well, well what do we have here?" a slightly familiar voice hisses from above. "Did the little mermaid come out to play?"

Freezing in my tracks, I look up to see one of the twins standing on the hatch. Pulling out Harmony, I widen my stance. "There's no game to be had here, but you will die this day."

A laugh echoes from the bow of the boat. "Get her, Jetsam, she's easy prey."

Before Jetsam can attack, I jump forward, holding the dagger ready to strike. In a rush of movement, he jumps over my head landing behind me. Oli engages him with his sword. The metal shrieks as the two tangle together. Waiting for a clean shot, I bob and weave with their movements. Storm is nowhere in sight, I can only hope he's assisting Wendell to take down the second twin.

Seeing my opportunity, I lunge forward, striking Jetsam on the shoulder. Blood stains his white shirt and he lets out a yell. In one jarring moment, he kicks Oli off the deck and pivots toward me with a grimace. Holding my position, I hold harmony in both hands. Without thinking, I begin to hum. The twin's eye glows and he raises his sword and brings it down swiftly, grazing my shoulder. The cut burns and I wince, taking a step back.

"Tit for tat," he taunts. "Do you really think you can beat me with that dagger?"

My hands are clammy as I raise Harmony in the air, humming louder. Flotsam cackles as he draws his sword upward, ready to attack. A rush of rage fills me and I run forward, screaming. I plunge Harmony into his chest with one hand and push him off the side of the boat with the other.

A splash sounds below and I lean over only to see his body transform into an eel and dart away. Holding my mouth with my hand, I scan the boat for the others. A clash of metal sounds out from the bow. Worried about Oli, I check the water behind the boat. Relief washes over me to see Oli climbing the ladder to the dock. Knowing he's safe, I quickly run toward the sound of the fight.

"Storm? Wendell?" I yell as the mist thickens.

No answer. The bow has become quiet. With a sick feeling settling in my stomach, I jump up to the mast and use it as a lookout point. Visibility is almost nothing as I pan from side to side. Biting my lip, I yell out for them again.

"Aye, over here lass," Wendell finally answers.

Sheathing my dagger, I drop down to the deck. A puddle of red leads me to the pirate, laying against the edge of the deck. My heart clenches and I drop to my knees. "No!"

Patting Wendell down, I search for the wound. Ripping at his shirt, a large gash in his side is revealed. Placing my hand over it, I fight to keep tears at bay. I don't know how to stop the blood from seeping out.

"Where's Storm?"

"The braided fellow took him overboard," Wendell wheezes. "Lend me that scarf and I'll wrap it around me side."

As quick as I can, I pull the fabric from my head and help Wendell wrap his side. When he seems stable, I stand up. Wiping blood on my pants, I run to the edge and look overboard to see a body floating beside the boat. With a strangled cry, I rip off my pants and dive into the water. My fin forms as soon as I submerge and I propel myself toward Storm's still body.

"Storm!" I yell as I turn him face up. His skin is pale and clammy. My lips trembling, I hoist him over my shoulder and drag him toward the dock.

"Oli, help me!" I call out.

Oli meets me at the stairs, leaning over and grabbing Storm. He lays him on the dock and begins pushing on his chest with both hands. Wendell joins his side and I dive back under the water to search for the twins.

Swimming under the boat, I grip Harmony at my side. I make my way from one end of the dock to the other, with no trace of the eels in sight. No living creature is in sight, all frightened away. The deep water calls me as if the twins left a beacon for me to follow. My head spins with indecision. Do I follow them or go back and check on the guys?

"You need them," Harmony makes the choice clear. Turning back to the dock with a tinge of regret, I sigh.

"Oi, there be a set of clothes up here," Wendell yells as I swim around the side, into his view.

Refusing to give up, I hold Harmony in my palm and hum. She vibrates for a solid minute before a vision forms before me. Jetsam stands on the deck watching as I appear. As soon as he sees me, he changes forms and flops into the water to join his brother as eels. The image fades as they seek shelter behind the pier.

"Why run if they want me dead?" I wonder out loud. "I have a feeling they're trying to lure me into the sea, thinking they'll catch me alone."

"A trap then?" Storm leans over the side, staring into the water.

"Most likely," I sigh as I hoist myself out of the water. Oli, saint that he is, hands me my pants before things get awkward.Sliding my damp legs inside, I fume. "But I must follow them. I can't let them get away with ruining my life!" I cry, trying to decide what to do next. "We should have come at night, it was stupid of me to stop and rest."

"How can they change forms? Where is their magic coming from if Eric killed the sea witch?" Storm asks.

"That's the question, isn't it?" I hold up Harmony, glaring at the ruby. "Tell me who is giving the twins their power."

She doesn't answer, nor did I really think that she would.

"Aye, Ari, never fear. We will get them next time." Wendell winces as he wraps an arm around my waist.

"We need to get you fixed up." I say, glancing up at him.

"'Tis but a scratch," he teases.

"Come on, I need you to be on the mend before we take on the twins again," I say as I slip from his grip.

He sighs and follows me off the boat.

"Can we burn this ship?" I ask, smiling toward my men. My question brings a smile to their lips.

"That's the best idea I've heard all morning," Storm replies.

"I'm sure there is some rum on board to help fuel the flames," Oli states with a little hopefulness. The three of us watch as he disappears back onto The Sea Witch and we all wait for him to reappear.

"Do you really think that those slimy eels drink?" Storm asks, with an eyebrow raised.

"Me thinks they may. Our girl, here, was a mermaid and she can drink like a fish," Wendell smirks.

Before I can say anything more on the matter, Oli shows up again. He is waving an amber bottle in each hand. Triumph is plastered on his face like an 'I told you so' expression.

"Good job," I say with a pat on his shoulder.

He hands me one of the bottles before he uncorks the other and takes a swig.

"Um, I thought we were using that to burn the boat?" I fold my arms.

"I'm getting to that," he laughs before ripping the bottom of his shirt and stuffing it in the bottle.

Oli had tucked some fuel tar spill into his boots and he removed it before walking to the closest lantern to light it.

Still smiling he lit the fabric that was hanging from the bottle before he threw it on the boat. Then he repeated with the second bottle but threw it on the opposite side.

The four of us stand there for a few minutes, watching as the boat drowns in flames. Oli and Storm run and untie the ropes that hold it to the docks and give it a little push. We couldn't have it taking out the dock when we had meant for just that ship to burn.

We turn and head back toward the town and the little inn where we had stayed. When we are about halfway up the dock, an explosion sounds behind us.

"Were there more bottles on that boat?" I ask, glancing at Oli.

"That and maybe some cannon powder," he smirks with a shrug.

That gets a laugh from all of us, until Wendell winces with pain.

"I be fine," he comments as he must have seen the concern on my face. "What about ye? I thought I noticed some blood on ye shoulder."

"It's nothing that can't wait to be taken care of until we get back and get you fixed up," I tell him.

But all three men stop, Oli takes a step behind me to try and examine it.

"I'm fine, it's Wendell we need to have looked at," I hiss, pulling from his grasp.

"Touchy much?" he comments as he moves around me and starts toward our destination once again.

Ignoring him, I take care with Wendell and he loops his arm over my injured shoulder. I do my best not to touch his wound and we limp on.

"What a pair we are, huh?" Wendell jokes.

"Nah, they cheated. We took them by surprise, sure. But all that fog had to come from somewhere," I comment, trying to remember if they had magic before. When I went to see the sea witch, they were in their eel form already. Were they under a curse like so many before them, but she took pity on them and made them her pets? "That was my error, I didn't think they would be more than men, and I won't make that mistake again."

There are a few people milling about, but it's still early, so we don't have to navigate too many bodies.

Wendell's breathing becomes labored the closer we get to the inn.

"I thought it was just a scratch?" I ask, glancing up at him.

"Aye, stop your worrying, woman." He smirks.

Was that sweat on his brow? He does seem a bit warm to the touch, but I'm still not sure how humans act when they're ill. Why would that cut cause an infection?

"We need to pick up the pace, I think there was more to those blades than we first thought," I say, biting my lip.

They don't question me, Oli stops in front of Wendell, "Climb on."

"Excuse me?" Wendell questions.

"Climb on my back. We will get to the inn faster if I carry you," he tells him.

"I will not," he retorts.

"Shut it, Wendell. Climb on and let's go," I order.

"Pushy much, lass?" he asks as he wraps his arms around Oli's neck and hooks his legs around his waist.

I shrug and we continue back on our way. Storm is at my side and we trail behind Oli and Wendell. It's amazing that it doesn't seem like it makes any difference in Oli's steps. I guess all that working in the forge helps with all that upper body strength. I had to remind myself not to drool and to focus on Wendell.

"Ari, are you okay?" Storm asks, eyeing me.

"What? I'm fine," I reply.

"You are paler than normal. Do you feel warm?" he asks as he takes a step closer towards me.

I wave his hand away, "Wendell, first. He was cut worse than I was. Whatever is wrong with him is the same for me. So, when he is fixed, I'll worry about me."

We are back at the inn when I finish my statement. Oli doesn't stop when the owners question us, he just keeps climbing the stairs to our room. He drops the pirate on the bed and with nimble fingers, I untie the scarf from around the wound. As I go to pull his shirt back, Oli puts his hands on mine.

I glance up at him and he gives me a weak smile. "Call the healer first. Best a professional be the one to touch whatever poison is in there."

ARI

Wendell lies in the bed, his face paler than I'd like. Storm left with Oli to fetch some food and the healer. My shoulder burns, but it's nothing I can't handle. Pacing the room, I stop to stare out the window.

"I should have stayed in that cell." I lean my head on the glass. "We're getting nowhere and now you're hurt."

"Don't say that, Ari," Wendell pushes himself to a seated position and pats the bed beside him. Head drooping, I slowly cross the room and sit gingerly on the edge of the bed. Wendell will have none of it, grabbing me by the waist and hoisting me close.

"This little sting is worth knowing ye. Don't worry so much, we'll catch those slippery fellas. They slid out of our hands for a purpose, that be sure."

Caving in and resting my head on his shoulder, I sigh. There's something I'm not seeing. I thought we'd planned the attack well enough, but I didn't expect the twins to be able to shift. The question is without the Sea Witch, how are they accessing power?

"There's no way to know who those two are

working for without following them into the sea. The only problem is I'll risk falling into a trap." I frown.

"Have ye thought about talking to yer Da?" Wendell tips my face to his.

Not wanting to think about my father, I close the distance and kiss him lightly. The door creaks open and the aroma of food fills the room. Perking up, I hop off the bed and cross the room. Storm steps in my path, a wry grin on his face.

"Where's my kiss?" He opens his arms.

Glad for the connection, I fall into his hold and lean my head back. His lips meet mine softly before urgency sets in and he clenches my bottom. Leaning closer, I wrap my arms around his neck and open my mouth for his tongue. My body lights on fire, need taking over any other discomfort I'm feeling.

"I'd say get a room," Oli opens the door, and Storm reluctantly lets me go, "but this is ours." He shakes his head as he ushers the healer inside. "This is Trinity," Oli points to the woman dressed in layers of purple.

A small part of me is embarrassed at how glad I am that Oli kept a wide berth from the healer. Stepping forward, I offer her my hand. She looks me over with trepidation before placing her palm against mine.

"I'm Ari," I shake. "Thank you for coming so quickly."

"Don't thank me until I have a look at this cut." Trinity lifts her skirt, crosses the room, and begins prodding at Wendell's side.

A wave of nausea hits me as I watch and I back up a

step. Storm catches me, slipping his arms around my waist for support.

"What do you think it is?" Oli moves material out of the wound while Trinity works.

"From the symptoms and minimal swelling, I'd guess sea snake venom. We'll need to clean the area and apply a bandage to keep the swelling down. Lucky for you we had another bloke poisoned just yesterday, so I've got anti-venom in my bag." Trinity looks at me with her nose scrunched. "I don't want to know what type of folk you're getting mixed up with, but I'd be wary of anyone resorting to tipping their blades. A sword is a fine killing weapon on its own, only a person up to worse than death uses poison."

"Aye," Wendell waves his hand. "Stop jabbering and fix me up so I can get back to me rum bottles."

Trinity shakes her head before opening her bag for supplies. I watch as Oli and Storm make a fire to heat water, not knowing how to help. Once the water is ready, we both get our wounds washed and bandaged. The last step is a draw of thick, purple liquid from a bottle Trinity produces. I gag, but swallow it down in the end.

"Ack," I wipe my mouth. "Where's that rum?"

Someone passes me a bottle and I take a drink. Oli passes coins to Trinity and she turns toward the door. "You've got a dark stain following you, beware it doesn't overtake ye," she says with a snarl to Oli before stomping out the door.

"Oi, that was harsh," Oli grabs his chest.

"Aye, but it be true in some ways." Wendell shakes his head. "Never fear, lass we'll complete the quest."

Relief floods my veins and I take a deep breath. "Well, now we're all fixed up. Time to get moving." I clap my hands.

"Uh, nope," Storm pulls out a chair. "You need to let that scab up before we head out again. Besides, those two things went into the sea, how are we supposed to fight them in the water?"

Defeated, I plop down beside Wendell and steal his rum again. The liquid burns less each time I take a drink. I know Storm is right, but I don't think I can just quit. There has to be a way to enact vengeance so that I may be free of the Dagger's push. I've held back sharing with the guys how much I think of killing throughout the day. I worry that the longer this takes, the less I will retain my own personality. Still, there is merit to resting.

"Fine. We'll head back to the Jolly Barnacle to rest. I can pick up Sebastian on the way. Maybe he can send a message to my father," I picture Triton's face of fury and wince. "It will have to be a well-worded message."

"Aye, 'tis a plan me can get behind." Wendell winks, bottle raised.

"Hey, you've had your alone time with Ari," Storm eyes me with heat. "Share and share alike."

"Now, that's a plan I can get behind." I blow a kiss at the tracker and smile.

Oli looks between the two men and shrugs. The bottle is passed around and we sit in front of the fire drinking for a while. The decision is made to stay at

SINGING DAGGER

the inn until dawn, since we've paid for the room, before heading back to the Jolly Barnacle. Oli slips out to order food and tell the owner we'll be leaving in the morning.

Oli's been a little distant since we fought the twins on the boat. Was there something that he wasn't telling me or was I just blowing nothing out of proportion?

"Aye, does anyone have a deck of cards?" Wendell asks with a hiccup.

"Cards? You can barely sit up, how are you going to play?" Storm asks with a laugh.

"This lass can hold my cards and I'll tell her how to play me hand." Wendell smirks, patting my good shoulder.

"What kind of card game are you talking about?" I ask as I get up to do that annoying human thing of relieving my bladder. If I would have known about these needs, I may have thought twice about leaving my fins behind.

"You don't want to play?" Wendell asks as I touch the doorknob.

"I'm game, but I need a moment to do those basic human things," I say, opening the door.

"What?" he questions, confusion written on his face.

"Bathroom, genius," Storm comments as I head out, leaving them to talk among themselves.

I don't hear many voices as I make my way down toward the bar. There is a bathroom on our floor but I want to check on Oli. I can't shake the feeling that something is off. When my feet hit the landing, I regret not grabbing Harmony before I left my two men.

"Are you sure it's not her?" a deep voice growls.

"Aye, she is not who you seek," Oli whispers.

I don't move a muscle. Are they talking about me?

"That red hair is a dead giveaway. Why are you protecting her, Oli?" the voice asks.

"Just because her locks are red, doesn't mean that she is who the twins want. My companion is a friend that Wendell met on one of his adventures. She was looking for a change of scenery and came back with him. He's hoping to talk her into sailing the seas with him," Oli replies.

That seems to appease the disembodied voice as a stool scrapes on the wooden floor and the footsteps grow lighter as they walk away from where I stand.

"Come out, Ari. I know you're there." My blacksmith sighs.

"How'd you know I was here?" I step out of the shadows toward him.

"Not many people give off the fragrance of lilies and brine." He shrugs with a half smile.

"So, you're saying I smell like a salty flower? I don't know if that's a compliment or insult. But that's a discussion for another time. Who were you talking with?" I raise an eyebrow.

"That was a terrible tracker from another village south. He heard rumors of a red-haired maiden here and wanted to see for himself. I told him there was such a woman here but not the princess he was seeking. After all we've been through, you don't trust me?" he asks with a slow, disbelieving head-shake.

I take a seat across from him, looking in his eyes the

entire time. "I swear to the Goddess of Vengeance, if you are two-timing me, not only will I kill you slowly, but cut your manhood off and feed it to you first."

"As you should," he says flatly. "But I swore an oath on your dagger to be with you on this quest. I am not one to go back on my word, Ari."

His words ring true and I feel a little better but I am still in need of going to the bathroom. Just as I am going to speak, the waitress brings over our food.

"Would you like for me to take this up to your room for you?" She smiles sweetly at Oli.

"Nah, my wife and I are more than capable of taking it up," he replies, gesturing to me.

Her face falls as she notices that I'm seated at the table, but she gives a small smile before excusing herself.

"If I didn't know any better, I'd think she wanted more than just to deliver your dinner," I smirk, my stomach in knots at the thought.

"Too bad, for her, that I'm a one gal kind of man." He shrugs.

"Do you hate that I won't pick you over the other two?" I ask honestly.

"If you need all three of us, then you get all three of us. Just know that we will be loyal to only you," he promises.

"That's more than I deserve," I say, lowering my face to stare at the table.

Oli leans over the table hooking two fingers under my chin to bring my gaze back to him, "As much as I'd love you all to myself, I'm here. If you say the three of us are yours because the Goddess guided you to us, how can I go against her wishes? Besides, you didn't ask for three men...or did you?" Oli smiles at me.

My cheeks flush a little, "I never asked for men at all, just justice to right the wrong."

He drops his hand to the table but not his gaze.

"Then, don't be so hard on yourself. Never doubt that I want to be with you. Not only that, but I will follow you anywhere," he crosses his arms over his chest.

"Thank you," is all I can choke out.

"We best get this up to Wendell and Storm before the food gets cold," Oli states, gesturing at the plates.

"I need a human moment first, that was the real reason that I came down here in the first place. Not to spy on you," I inform him

"I'll be right here when you get back," he promises, not looking away from me.

The floor seems to disappear as I walk slowly away from Oli. I hope the other two feel as strongly as he does. The more I'm with the guys, the more I know I could never live without them. As quickly as I can, I slip into the bathroom and handle the awful business. When I emerge, Oli's smile is the first thing I see. Glad for the small moment together, I grab a plate and we head back to the room.

Storm and Wendell are suspiciously quiet when we enter, but I brush it aside. As if we're all plotting, we shovel the food in our mouths quietly. The best part is that Wendell is starting to get some color back.

"Now it be time for cards," he declares as he pushes his plate away.

"What kind of game are you thinking, Wend?" I ask as I place my plate on top of his and move them to the hall.

"Why strip poker, of course," he smirks.

"Well, if I'm playing your hand, you have to strip and so will these other guys. I didn't realize that you were so keen on getting them naked," I say.

His face falls as he realizes the flaw in his plan.

"Maybe just regular poker it be."

ARI

Sitting on the bed next to Wendell, I hold his cards in my hand. Storm and Oli sit on either side of the bed, peering from face to face as they contemplate the game. It amuses me how hard they try to out play one another. Little by little I'm picking up on the rules, but, honestly, I'm having more fun just watching the show.

"All in." Wendell points to our stack of coins. Trying to keep my face calm, I push them into the middle of the mattress.

"Are you trying to dip out of the game early?" Storm raises an eyebrow.

"When have I ever backed out of a chance to take ye money?" Wendell grins.

Oli laughs, laying his cards down. "I fold."

Storm sits up straight, eyeing his hand. After a few whispers to himself, he pushes his coins into the pot as well. "I'll see your bet."

"Aye, lay the cards down, Ari," Wendell's grin widens.

Shaking my head, I place a ten, nine, eight, seven,

and six of hearts on the bed. Storm leans forward in his chair, his face unreadable. After stalling a moment, he places four twos and a joker beside Wendell's cards.

"Oi, Storm wins the hand," Oli barks as he slaps his leg. Storm winks my way as he drags the coins toward him. "Time to call it a night. We've got some traveling ahead of us in the morning. Going over land, it'll be a long day."

"That's true. Uh, Ari?" Oli leans back in his chair, his cheeks flaming. I scoot toward him, wondering what's up. It takes him a moment of shuffling before he finally speaks. "Since Wendell cannot be shuffled around, I took it upon myself to grab two more rooms for the night. I was wondering if you'd like to join me?"

Biting my lips, I look over to Wendell who tilts his head toward the blacksmith. "Aye, lass, go take the time with Oli. I be needing rest, and Storm will survive a night without ye as well."

Storm puckers his lips but nods. "It's fair for us each to have alone time with you. I call tomorrow night, though." He almost pouts, which makes me giggle.

"I talked to Oli already, but I need to hear it from you two as well." I steeple my fingers. "Can you handle the fact that I won't choose between you? I promise there will be no others, but the Goddess sent me to you three for a purpose and I won't give any of you up. I've lost all I can handle," I stop as tears threaten to fall.

"Aye, I be firm on what ye be needing from us." Wendell taps my leg. "We belong to ye."

"I can handle these two if you can." Storm's stern look quickly fades into a smile that lights up his eyes.

The knot in my stomach unravels and I take a deep breath. "Okay. I know it's not fair, but I can't abide by another woman in our group," I grit my teeth.

"How could anyone compete with you?" Oli kneels at my feet.

"There isn't a more beautiful, strong, determined woman in all of Tirulia," Storm stands, taking my hand.

"Lass, ye be the finest booty around," Wendell states with a sideways grin.

Shaking my head, I slide off the bed. Leave it to the pirate to lighten the mood. Glad for the chance to escape a long talk with tears, I blow him a kiss. Oli lobs a key over to Storm, then takes my hand and leads me out of the room.

"That was painless." He squeezes my hand.

"Thankfully." I smile.

We take a left down the hall and follow it to the end. Oli opens the door, holding it for me. As soon as I step over the threshold, my insides twist into knots again. Things with Wendell happened so spur of the moment, I didn't think about being nervous, but tonight? My cheeks flame as I stare at the bed. The door clicks behind us and Oli clears his throat.

"I don't expect anything but your time," he whispers as he leads me across the room.

I giggle. "Ah, so your evil plan was to get me alone to talk?" I turn and face the blacksmith. His dark hair has fallen over one eye, giving him a more mysterious look. The moonlight filtering in the window makes his blue eyes look like pools of silver. A shiver runs up my spine as I close the distance between us.

"Ari," Oli cups my jaw.

There are no more words. The attraction between us becomes nuclear. Our lips meet and I melt into him. Oli's kiss is hesitant, and ever so delicate. Needing more, I wrap my arms around his neck and rise to my tiptoes. I coax Oli into a deeper kiss, one that hints at the fulfillment I so badly need. Oli groans as he fidgets with the buttons on my shirt. Stepping back, I undo the buttons with ease as I pin him with a heated gaze. A quiet sensuality brews within Oli, stoking the flame of my desire.

Cold air dances on my skin as I peel my pants off. When I look back up, Oli stands before me clothed only in the night. His taut, steely muscles ripple as he stalks toward me. Gone is the hesitancy, Oli's eyes hold a glint of possession.

"You are more beautiful each time I look at you," he breathes as our lips meet again. This time, the heat is undeniable as it engulfs us.

Welcoming him with an open-mouthed kiss, I crawl onto the bed, taking him with me. Oli captures me in his sinewy arms, his erection cushioned against my abdomen. Anticipation so keen lights through me and I urge him onward, arching my hips against him. His smoky scent envelops me, adding to the burn I feel.

"Please, Oli," I mew.

"Ari, this will not be fast. I intend to savor every second." Oli's lips leave mine.

His eyes slit to half-mast as he takes a long look at my body. Wriggling under his penetrating gaze, I attempt to lure him back. Oli kisses me playfully before planting more kisses from my breasts to my navel. Devastating my control, he dips down between my thighs with his mouth. His greedy mouth takes bold possession of my mound and a long, liquid sea of pleasure rolls from my core to my head, leaving me breathless.

Spasms of pure, unadulterated release lash over me. Oli's tongue dips and swirls around my clit, driving me mad. Undulating in his tight grip, I whimper for what I don't know. The onslaught of ecstasy is almost unbearable. Never have I had a man focus on me in this way. Just when I think I might explode, Oli lets up, allowing me to breathe. Wildness flickers beneath his gentleness as he kisses down my leg to my ankle. Gooseflesh breaks out along his path.

"Your skin is so soft," he breathes as he makes his way back toward my navel. His hot breath teases at my wetness, but continues moving north.

My nipples become his next focus. Writhing beneath Oli's ministrations, I take a moment to admire the full length of his powerful physique. His strength doesn't match with the gentle way he coaxes my body to fulfillment.

"Oli," I gasp. "Please take me."

Oli's eyes spark and he settles his body over mine. Arching my hips toward his jutting erection, my legs quiver. Oli grips my ass with one hand as his shaft nudges against my opening. The anticipation is so keen I almost explode before he enters. When he finally inches his way in, I gasp as his girth stretches me more than I was ready for. A delicious fullness replaces the gaping need that clawed at me and I throw my hands over my head.

Oli's mouth takes possession of mine as he probes in a slow, repetitive rhythm. The potency of his kiss is like a narcotic that I never want to quit. Grasping his hair, I languish in the feel of our bodies in one long, slow kiss. Before I know it, a shattering climax locks my legs and I growl.

"Oh fuck," Oli grits. His hands clench the sheets near my head and his thrusts become more urgent. Our bodies rock together as fireworks light beneath my eyelids. My nipples harden and a volcanic explosion rocks my core. Oli cries out, plunging into the hilt as he spills his seed. His arms tremble as he holds his body still over mine, raining kisses over my chin.

"Ari," he gasps as he falls over beside me. "I'm sorry I meant to pull out."

My head spins for a moment as I think of the implications of his words. I almost panic before I realize I've been taking precautions since I was married. "No, it's okay. I won't get pregnant," I lift my head with one hand and stare at his sweat-soaked body. He's more sexy like this than should be legal. Oli releases a breath and tugs me toward him for another light kiss. I sink into his hug and relish in the intimacy.

"Do you think we'll find them?" he whispers as we look out the window.

"We have to," I conjure an image of Moryana and shiver with a different sort of need.

Oli and I settle next to each other, content with just each other's company, words aren't needed.

"Ari," Harmony calls.

In my haste to be near Oli, I tossed her on the floor without a thought, until now.

"Ari, 'tis time. Moryana requests you to seek vengeance in her name."

I groan as I rummage through my clothes until my hand meets the cool steel of Harmony's grip. Her ruby is glowing.

"Just me or my men as well?" I ask, before glancing back to Oli.

"You may take one, but he must not interfere with your quest. You have to make the kill, my blade must taste the blood," Harmony commands.

Oli moves towards the end of the bed, drawing closer to the blade and me.

"I can't believe that blade really talks to you." His jaw hangs open.

"Aye, and we have a mission. I made a bargain with the Goddess that blessed me with this blade. Her vengeance must be enacted along with mine. Get dressed, it can only be the two of us." I pull my shirt over my head.

"Wendell and Storm won't agree to this," he says, stepping into his pants.

"Be that as it may, Harmony, said one man. I can go grab Storm to come with me, if you don't want to join me," I taunt, as I right my pants to where they belong

"I never said I wouldn't go, but I left my blade in the other room. Am I to go empty handed?" he asks.

"Aye," Harmony agrees.

"Harmony says yes. So, you ready?" I ask as I

rummage through the room, searching for something to hide my hair in. The last drawer I come to saves me from having to return to the former room. Wendell would ask questions and I haven't the time to explain. There's an urgency running through me that I can't deny. Pulling the scarf from the drawer, I step toward the mirror and quickly bind my hair.

Oli comes up behind me and pulls me to him, he sweeps my concealed hair to one side and places gentle kisses on the other.

"Normally, I would welcome the distraction. But if we don't do this for the Goddess, I will never end those that did this to me," I say in a whisper.

"Well, we can continue this later." He drops one last kiss before moving away from me.

"I'd enjoy that. Now let's leave before I lose my nerve," I say, heading for the door.

We are on the road in no time, I wait until there are no eyes on me to pull Harmony from my waist. Placing her in both palms, I begin her favorite tune and in return she begins to glow as she spins, that is until she stops.

"This way," I tell Oli. "Harmony says we are to go north."

I place Harmony in one hand and take Oli's in the other. We follow where Harmony leads, her hilt warming my palm, until we veer off course.

"We are heading out of town, are you sure we haven't gone too far?" Oli asks, a little confusion in his tone.

"I know it's hard to believe, but my blade will not

steer us wrong. She has yet to," I promise as I pull him left on the road.

"This leads to the Sparrow manor. Is that who we are after?" he asks.

"She didn't tell me a name. Just that it was time," I answer honestly.

"Okay, does she have a plan or anything to tell us?" he questions.

"Shh, we're getting close. If you don't shut it soon, I may miss the mark," I chide.

Oli doesn't say anything, but squeezes my hand and I take that as he understands.

"He is close," Harmony hisses. *"Keep your guard up, leave the man. He should wait in the shadows. You won't be able to get near the target if you're not alone."*

"You must wait in the shadows. It's the only way I can get close to the target. You needn't be far just not seen," I say, trying to reassure him that I'm not going to do anything stupid. Well, mostly. I've never stalked a man to kill. "And do not hold whatever I say or do against me, I have to be close enough to stab him in the heart."

Oli stares at me, then at the ruby glowing at Harmony's hilt. With a sigh he gives in. "Aye, you'll just have some making up to do later." He winks as he lets go of my hand to slink into the shadows.

Twenty paces after I leave Oli, a figure comes into view. Thank goodness for the lamps that lit this passage toward the manor.

"Who's there?" a gruff voice calls.

"Oh, thank goodness, he won't stop following me," I

run toward the stranger, looking behind me as if I am scared. "Even now, he lurks in the shadows," I say with a tear sliding down my cheek.

"What man? I don't see anyone," he says as I move closer toward him. Harmony burns my palm, telling me all I need to know. He is my mission.

As if on cue, Oli rustles some leaves and I pretend to be startled.

"See, that's him," I cry.

The man draws me near, wrapping an arm around me as I had hoped. It's all I can do to stifle a shiver of disgust as he pulls me to him.

"I won't let him hur…" is all he gets out before I plunge Harmony straight into his heart. The dagger vibrates in contentment when I remove her from his chest. The body falls to the dirt with a thud.

"Oli! We have to get rid of this body," I say motioning.

"Sure, sure you get all the fun and I have to clean up the mess," he jokes, stepping out of the shadows.

"I am still a princess," I shrug. Which gets a laugh from him.

"So, you're used to people cleaning up after you?" he questions.

"Nah, I have too many messes for that," I wink.

Oli lifts the man over his shoulder with ease and starts towards the sea.

"No fire this time?" I ask, following behind him.

"If someone starts to look into all the people and bodies piling up, best not to use the same method every time," he replies. I nod, though he can't see me. It's good that he came or I'd be fumbling around trying to burn the guy.

"I take it you've thought about this a lot?" I question as the grass turns to sand under my feet. The faster I try to walk to keep up with Oli, the more I seem to trudge and kick the sand.

"As a blacksmith, you'd be surprised what people talk about when you're fixing their blades," he states as he walks into the water.

I don't follow him, transforming now would be useless without a reason to do so. But the sea calls to me. Even though I shake it off tonight, I know there will be a day that I will give in.

"You alright, Ari?" Oli lets the body down into the water. He bends over grabbing rocks and tucking them into the man's clothing. Then he pushes the body out to sea and watches it sink before he wades back ashore.

"I am, but I'd say it's time for another bath to get this adventure off our skin," I say, looping my arm in his once he is on land again.

"That I can get behind," he says as we start the trek back to this little inn. I smile to myself, noticing how Oli's shyness seems to have disappeared.

ARI

Golden fingers of sunlight light up the sky as we come back to the inn. The just-risen sun shines softly on the city streets, bringing with it a flurry of early-morning activity. Ducking out of sight, Oli and I cross the common room and head for the stairs. The tension in his hands belies the coolness he radiated while on the mission.

"I'm going to need to stop by my cave near the Jolly Barnacle for more jewels. I can't keep wearing the cast off rags that we find along the way," I complain.

Oli looks down at me before nodding. "It would do us all some good to fetch proper clothing. We'll call unwanted attention looking like guttersnipes. I've got credit at the seamstress near my shop, we'll go there once we travel home. The girl that works there is fair friends with my ma, so she'll keep her lips locked about our patronage."

"Okay. Maybe Storm can rustle up a dress for me to wear in the meantime," I say as I open the door to Wendell's room. Storm has beat us there, standing at the fireplace with a hand on his hip.

"Enjoy yourselves?" He turns around and produces a kettle.

"Uh," Oli reddens. "It was a fair evening."

Ignoring the banter between the two, I step toward the bed. "How are you feeling today?" I lean down and place a kiss on Wendell's cheek.

"Fit as a fiddle," the pirate pats his bandage. "Nothing for ye to worry about. Although, I could use a scrubbin'." He sniffs his underarm with disgust.

"Same," Storm frowns. "Guess I should go down into town and find more clothing?" He eyeballs the dark stain on my shirt. I sigh, feeling caught in a loophole of sending the men for food and clothing at every turn. What I wouldn't give to have a simple life for once.

"I'll come with you," Oli digs through the pile of clothing we have in the room, finds a passable shirt and tugs it on. I'm surprised he bothered, the man seems to run around bare chested more than anything. He and Storm exit without another word spoken, leaving me with Wendell the stinky pirate.

"Looks like Storm was busy this morning," I comment as I notice steam rising from the tub.

"Aye, he made coffee and had the bath drawn before the sun was ready to shine," Wendell winces as he rises from the bed.

Worried I rush over, lending him an arm as he makes his way across the room. I wish I were a witch, and not just a mermaid with a magical dagger. Then I could heal Wend and get rid of the twins without anyone else getting hurt. Annoyed with the status quo,

I unravel the bandage at Wendell's waist. It sticks a little where the blood dried but my mouth drops open when I look at the wound.

"Call me crazy, but that looks a lot better than I was hoping." I move his arm out of my way as I inspect the area.

"Let me see yours," Wendell bats me away, pulling down the neckline of my shirt..

"You just want me out of my shirt again," I tease.

"Aye, that I'll always welcome." He chuckles. "Yer cut is naught but a scrape now. That healer must have used black magic." Wendell spits on the ground.

My heart thumps as I recall my run-in with the late sea witch. Shaking my head, I turn away. "No, black magic wouldn't help us. Maybe Harmony helped," I shrug. "Either way, we're well enough to get back on the road. Strip out of those awful rags and get in the water. I'll help you wash."

Wendell eyes me for a long minute before stripping and stepping into the tub. Lathering up a rag, I bend toward him when a seagull's squawk catches my attention. Handing the towel to Wendell, I walk to the window and open it wide.

"Ari!" Scuttle yells. "I've been searching all over for you!"

"How ever did you find me here?" I step back as he lands on the windowsill.

"Wait…. Ari. Are ye talking to that bird?" Wendell splashes as he turns in the tub.

Fidgeting, I look from Scuttle to Wendell. "Uh, it kind of comes with the whole mermaid thing." I dip my head. I can't imagine how weird things must be from his point of view.

"Aye," Wendell's eyes go wide and he turns back around, dunking his head.

"Do you have news for me?" I ask as I shuffle over to the tub to check on my guy.

"The place you were staying in was raided. They almost killed Sebastian, but he escaped. A stray dog helped the crab get back to your cave where he met up with Flounder. Flounder came to find me and I've been searching for you since. You can't go back to Tirulia, kid there are soldiers and mercenaries everywhere!" Scuttle flaps his wings dramatically.

My heart sinks as I reach in and grab Wendell's hair, pulling him out of the water. He comes up sputtering and swearing.

"Aye, gimme a minute, lass! Me thinks the sight of ye having a black fin and not being gobsmacked should be commended. Ye never spoke of talking to sea rats!" Wendell's voice raises an octave.

"I'm sorry, it's been a fast-paced few days." I cup his jaw. "Everything that comes with me is a lot, I know. You can stay behind if you want, I won't think badly of you for it."

"Arrgh, ye know that's not what me be meaning." Wendell swats at my hand. "Fetch me a towel, I don't want the dangly bits wavin before ye feathered friend."

Stifling back a laugh, I hold out a towel for the pirate. He rises, wrapping the towel around his waist before stepping out of the tub. "What he be squawking about then?"

SINGING DAGGER

"I can't go back to Tirulia, they've found our room at the Harpy," I sigh.

"Blimey, we've got to get the Jolly Barnacle out of the dock before they track ye to the ship!" Wendell mutters as he scrounges through the clothing, sniffing each piece before casting it back to the floor.

The door opens. Storm and Oli enter laden with packages. Setting them on the bed, Storm turns toward me. "We got enough supplies for a week. No more living day to day."

"That's good. I've got bad news." I point to Scuttle.

The eccentric seagull squawks and goes into some spiel, but I'm ignoring him as Storm and Oli raise a brow at the bird.

"Scuttle, please," I beg, I love that bird but he's starting to make my head hurt. He quiets as I tell the two that just walked in the news.

"Well, what's our next move?" Oli asks, "Do we split up? Ari, you said you were in need of more jewels and clothing. Storm and I could procure that and meet back up with you and the pirate."

"No," Harmony says.

"Harmony doesn't want us apart. So, we stick together. We will have to find another way to the cave," I shrug, discouraged with this turn of events.

"Aye, I can cover all coins and credits we need," my pirate speaks up.

"I will pay back anything we use," I promise.

"Aye, there be other ways ye can compensate me," Wendell says with a wink.

"How about you two change into the new clothes.

Storm and I will go downstairs and gather as much intel as possible. We should be ready to head out as quickly as a cat running on a hot roof," Oli says.

Storm grumbles something under his breath as he heads out with Oli.

"What's his problem?" I ask, turning back to my pirate.

"Aye, just a little sore he be the last to get you alone. He be fine, maybe just stick a little closer to his side today," he tells me.

"Unless you need me," I remind him. "Don't overdo it, I need you to finish this mission and longer."

As tough as the pirate may put off, my words pull a slight smile from his lips. "Aye, and ye be stuck with me."

"Ari," Scuttle squawks at me, reminding me that he is still here.

I turn toward him, "Yes, I know you're still there, my feathered friend. Can you please go find Flounder and make sure all is well under the sea. We will be on the move so you may have to search for us. If there is anything wrong, please come back immediately."

"Yes, Princess," he says with a little nod.

I have to contain a little laugh as Scuttle starts to screech his song as he disappears into the sunrise.

"He be the oddest bird I've had the pleasure of meeting," Wendell comments.

"Oh Scuttle. He holds a special place in my heart. That bird was my first surface friend." I shrug as I pick up some of the clothing the guys brought in. "Let's get you changed."

A smirk tips Wendell's lips, "If ye be wanting to touch me body, just say that, darling. No pretenses."

"Har, har, har. If we had time, I would really show you which of us is really in control." I wink as I throw a shirt at him. "I thought with your side you may want some help, but if not, that's up to you. I will check over the room and make sure that we don't leave a trace behind. With Storm's mood, I think that we best be ready to leave as soon as he and Oli return."

"Aye, if the guards are near, we best be on the move. We be outnumbered for sure," he comments.

My heartbeat increases with his words, what was I thinking when I escaped? The details about this mission were thrown to the wayside. Why hadn't I thought about the number of guards on my trail? Or that we may not be able to go back to my cave or rescue Sebastian. I have been so stuck on revenge that red is all I could see. Now that I have a little time to stop and think correctly, I've been a fool. I mean, we aren't leaving a chain of bodies in our wake. I will have to make sure that we keep our tracks covered as we have. No crumbs to lead them to us. Moryana promised me vengeance, does that include not getting caught? Need to be on my best behavior just to be on the safe side.

I had busied myself searching each and every one of the corners in this room when I hear a moan of pain from behind me.

I turn to Wendell and he has new trousers on but he can't seem to get them buttoned. "You stubborn pirate, I offered you help. Would you like some now?"

His scowl turns into a smile, "Aye, me shoulder be a little more tender then I imagined."

Standing, I place the items that I have gathered on the bed before taking the fabric from my pirate. My fingers skim over his abs and he wiggles a little as if it tickles, but I take care not to touch his wound.

"I thought you were helping," he comments.

"I am," I say, glancing up into his chestnut eyes. "Not my fault if you're ticklish."

I do my best not to lightly touch him as I fasten his pants and help him slip on his shirt. I'm to the last button when the handle of the door jiggles, announcing the return of Storm and Oli. I jump back from Wendell as if we have been caught, but then I have to laugh at myself. I think Storm's moodiness has me on edge and I don't want to lose him. I need him and not just because the dagger says so, it's something I feel in my soul.

"Aye, welcome back. Took you long enough," Wendell jokes.

"Yeah, thanks," Storm grouches, throwing a package on the bed. "There's not much to tell. The townspeople have all clammed up. But we did find you a nicer dress than when we wore out the first time. Shopping was a better cover than needling folks for information."

"I appreciate you," I say with a weak smile as I lift the parcel with care. Wendell's words about giving Storm a little more attention today ring in my ears. "Storm, would you mind helping me dress?"

"Are you sure, Princess?" he asks stiffly, a little bit of coolness in his tone.

SINGING DAGGER

"Aye, Oli, let us take leave. I have a need for some rum," Wendell says, heading for the door.

There are no words as the two of them shuffle from the room and the door creaks closed behind them. Now, it's just Storm and I, standing there in awkward silence.

STORM

A war has been raging inside of me since the day Ari stepped up to my door. Part of me can't believe I agreed to go on this whirlwind of a quest, and the other can't believe I've lived a second of my life without her in it. How has she burrowed so deep within me? What is it about her? Beating myself up with questions has made me unreasonably cranky.

"Storm?" Ari's voice is laced with fear. I feel it, even if she's hid it from the others. Deep inside, she's quaking and it's tearing me apart.

"Yes?" I face her, my teeth gritted together.

"I'm sorry if you've felt left on the outside. I never meant that." She takes my hand and I clasp her fingers tightly.

"While part of me has felt that way," I sigh, "my edginess has more to do with worrying over you."

Ari's eyes widen, deepening the blue hue. "Me?"

Shaking my head, I unravel the parcel and hold up the dark-blue shift I've found. It will help Ari blend into the crowd versus stand out as a pirate or a princess. "Yes, you. I can feel your fear and I hope that you know I'm here for you. Can you just be real and honest with me? How are you not quaking in your boots every minute of every day? You've been changing, in small increments—but I'm worried. Is it the dagger?"

Ari holds her breath, lips sealed.

"I'm dying inside right now because I can't come to terms with how easily I've let you slip into my soul although I know so very little about you beyond folklore and blood," I tear away from her. "And yet I want you. I want you from the very root of my being to tell me you'll never leave my side. How is this normal?"

A low chuckle steals my heart. "Normal?" Ari steps into my sight. "Nothing about my life has been normal in the last few years. I went from almost dying by the hand of a sea witch to losing my husband, to some other evil force yet to be named. Yes, I was warned that the dagger would change me—which is yet another thing on my plate. Storm, I am terrified— yet, I have no choice but to push forward. I need you to keep me from falling apart. I don't know this human world as you do." She steps so close our noses meet. "Please."

Her body melts into mine and everything else is eclipsed. In a frenzy, we shed clothing. There's nothing romantic in the way that I mount her, to which I'm a bit ashamed, but Ari doesn't seem to care at the moment. Deciding to make it up to her later, I lavish her mouth with a long, deep kiss. Her legs wrap around me, urging me to keep moving. Ari's eyes pull me in, mesmerizing me with their ocean hue.

"Don't think, just be present right now," she whispers in my ear.

The aching tension that has been building between us floods the room like a tidal wave. Rocking the headboard against the wall, I break the waves the only way I know how. Keening mewls from below me are the only anchor as I thrust deeply into her velvety core.

"Oh, Storm," Ari moans and I come unglued.

Ari's thighs tighten and her body trembles beneath me. Holding my breath, I watch her enticing form as she throws her head back. Her face is flushed, plush lips open in a soft moan as she comes. Every pulse of her ecstasy translates through her body and into me. The little restraint I had left is torn away and I plunge into a frenzy of thrusts.

"Ari," I cry as my body tightens before its final release. Pulling out, I empty my seed into the sheets beside her, clenching the bedpost until my hand is sore.

Panting, I turn my head toward Ari. She smiles sweetly before sliding off the bed and tiptoeing to the water basin to clean herself.

"Aye, you two better be hurrying," Wendell's voice calls through the door. "I think our time is up here."

"Just a minute!" Ari laughs as she throws my pants at me.

There's a comical moment as we dash around gathering clothing. I open the parcel, holding the new underthings and dress. She scoffs at the bra, but it's not like we've got mermaid clams lying around. In silence, we dress. Although I'm on cloud nine, my mind is finally quiet for once.

When she finally turns back to me, my breath catches. The simple dress somehow makes her look more elegant than a ballgown might. Taking the black lace shawl, I create a veil to cover her head. She plants a small kiss on my lips before tucking Harmony neatly at her side and tying another shawl at her waist to hide the holster.

"Off we go," She sighs. "I promise the next night we are free from running will be ours." Ari opens the door, revealing an amused pirate and blacksmith leaning against the wall like a couple of perverts.

Shaking my head, I throw my bag over my head and lead the way down the stairs. When we were out, there was a thickness in the atmosphere. Following my gut, I turn at the bottom of the stairs and head out the back. As we exit the inn, my hunch is confirmed. A troop of soldiers marches along the main road. Narrowly escaping them, we travel down the back alley toward the docks. The only way out of here is by ship, which means we will either need to bribe someone or steal a vessel.

"To the docks?" Oli questions as we run.

"Aye," Wendell agrees. "Me thinks there was a fine-looking skiff we could borrow at the front of the dock."

"Steal you mean?" Ari frowns, but keeps moving.

"Lass, time is of the essence. It can be recovered by the owner once we get me ship."

"Okay," she agrees.

We run the last stretch along the cliff, not taking any chances with the roadside. The skiff Wendell has his eye on is a dilapidated, old fishing boat that is covered in dust and spider webs. Not asking any questions, we follow his lead and before long, we're off into the sea.

Ari has a look of concern on her brow as the dock disappears and the ocean is all that is on our horizon.

I move a little closer to her, "Princess, a coin for your thoughts?"

"I'm not sure, this just feels all wrong. The ocean used to be welcoming but now it is menacing and vast. How can your home change so much that you don't recognize it?" she asks in a small voice.

Not sure if I should pull her in or not, I've never been one that was good at really reading emotions but I don't have to. She leans her head on my shoulder and I wrap an arm around her waist.

"Your home is with the three of us. No matter where we are, never forget we are your home," I whisper and place a kiss on her forehead.

"Shiver me timbers, that was the sappiest thing I be hearing in a long time," Wendell teases.

"Shut it, Pirate," Ari states with a smirk.

"To the Jolly Barnacle then?" Wendell winks in return.

"As fast as we can manage," she nods.

"Aye, aye, Ari," Wendell says as he pulls the wheel and the boat turns.

Ari smiles up at me. I run a finger down her cheek and notice there is yet another tattoo on her gorgeous body. We were in the throes of passion before, so I wasn't scanning every inch of her like now.

"When did this pop up?" I question, skimming over the black ink on her shoulder.

"Oli and I may have taken a little excursion last night," she squeaks. "I told you when I took the dagger that I was not only on a quest for my revenge but that the Goddess has some things I agreed to do in repayment. So, we took a walk, killed a man and hid his body," she says lightly.

"Aww a nice stroll and murder, that makes for a wonderful night out," I joke.

Ari relaxes in my arms a little as the boat rolls on the little waves.

"Ari-el," a voice calls from a distance, we all perk up and scan the seas to see where the sound was coming from.

"Ari-el," it calls again but closer.

"Did you three hear my name as well?" Ari asks, glancing at us.

"Aye," we say at once.

"Impossible, Eric was never able to hear Sebastian speak," she comments as she runs to the other side of the deck.

"Storm, grab a bucket or something that we can use to raise Sebastian to the deck," Ari orders without taking her eyes off the waves.

There's not much on this skiff, but they did leave the net.

"Give me a minute, I have to fix a hole so he doesn't fall out before I can throw this overboard for him," I tell her as I set to work.

My fingers fumble with the coarse ropes but it

doesn't take me long to get the net in a workable condition. I jump up and head to where Ari is still standing and throw the net into the ocean.

"Sebastian, is it?" I call into the great blue ocean, "Climb into the net and I'll hoist you up to the ship."

"You can't see him can you?" Ari asks.

"No, but if you say he's out there, then I know he is."

Oli stands on the other side of Ari, scanning the waves as well.

"There he is," she calls, pointing to a red blur just on the end of the net.

Oli helps me heave the heavy ropes up and the little crab climbs over my shoulder and into Ari's open palms.

Tears stream down her cheeks as she pulls him closer to her. "I'm so sorry I left you in that hotel room. Scuttle told me what they did to you."

"Ari, none of this was your fault. I have informed your father and he has set up guards around his sea kingdom. He also wanted to come here himself but thought it was best not to call anymore attention to you. King Triton sends his love and wants you to know that if you need him, you only need to slip into the seas and call his name," the little, red sidekick tells her.

"Oh, Sebastian. I don't know if Father would recognize me. My fins, they are no longer the pearly green they once were. This dagger has not just charged me with a mission but changed who I am inside and out," she tells him.

"Ari girl, your father will always know you. He set you free to be with the man you love even when it killed him a little too much to do so. No matter what, he will always be in your corner. Is there anything you need from me?" Sebastian asks.

"Can you please search for whispers of the sea witch's eels? They are behind this, at least they are at the heart of it. My quest will end with them," she tells him.

"Ending them may be the end of your quest, but the beginning of a new journey, I see," he says as scans the three of us on the boat.

"How is it that I can hear you?" I ask him, still a little freaked out that I can talk to a crab.

"For my bravery, the King blessed me with this gift. I knew if Ari had any more adventures, it would be handy to be able to not only talk to her but any humans I see fit," he says.

"Smart thinking, Sebastian. Please thank my father and thank you once again for everything. Go back to the ocean, heal and I'll see you again soon," Ari promises.

"Thar be me lovely ship," the pirate calls from the wheel behind us. "Be ready to tie this skiff up and jump aboard quickly. We best set back as soon as we can."

Sebastian gives the three of us a little nod and jumps back into the water, I watch until he is a little, red blob under the current.

ARI

Thanks to the gods, the wharf is silent when we drift up to the pier. The berth two slots away from the Jolly is free, so Wendell takes it. As soon as we're close enough, Storm jumps off the deck and begins to tie the skiff to the dock. The rest of us scramble to gather our supplies and debark. In a matter of minutes, we boarded the Jolly Barnacle.

"Aye, the winds be shifting in our favor, no soldiers in sight." Wendell steps up to the wheel. "Ye three think ye can handle the Jolly? Me crew is still on break and risking searching for them sounds like a bad idea."

"We have to," I look from him to the dock. "Just tell me what to do and I'll pitch in."

"We all will," Oli agrees, already helping Storm bring in the plank.

It takes a lot of yelling and running, but we slide into a fair routine. My stress level doesn't let up until the banks of Tirulia are nothing but a green blurb in the distance. Climbing up the stairway to the poop deck, I wish I hadn't asked for a dress.

"Lass, we be far away from land but what heading

ye be wanting to take?" Wendell searches the horizon as if a huge sign would appear to mark our path.

"I guess I'd better consult Harmony," I sigh, more nervous than ever about using her magic.

Turning toward the water, I take a deep breath. Everything comes down to this. My hand trembles as I close my fingers around Harmony's grip. The sky darkens, dampening the whole vibe of the ship. Raising Harmony in my flattened palm, I look over to the guys who are gathered around the wheel. Each man nods, their eyes fixed on the ruby.

"Ah, ah, ah …" I begin the tune that's changed my life more than I dare to count.

The ruby flares to life and the blade begins to vibrate. The now-familiar red haze fills the air around me. Instead of spinning, Harmony once again offers a vision. When I see my father's face materialize, I drop the dagger on the deck.

"No, that can't be right," I gasp.

"Ari?" Storm grips my elbow while Oli retrieves Harmony from the floor.

Looking into Storm's eyes, my throat tightens. "That was my father. I don't understand why he was in the vision. It couldn't have been him that sent the twins to kill Eric, it just couldn't."

"We don't know that the vision holds who murdered Eric," Oli peers into the red stone. "Maybe he's the key to you finding the twins. Or does he have answers we need?"

"Harmony?" I plead but the blade is silent.

"King Triton it is then," I whisper. "Head north until the waters turn a dark navy blue."

Wendell taps me on the shoulder before heading back to the wheel. The ship lurches to the side as the bow aligns north and I strain to keep my balance. Oli wraps one arm around my waist and slides Harmony back into the scabbard at my hip. For a moment, I don't feel the thirst of the blade. In its place, there's a hollowness and fear of what's yet to come.

"Maybe you should rest?" Oli whispers.

"No, I have to be here when we breach King Triton's waters. Otherwise, we'll face a storm."

"I'll rustle up some food then," Storm heads down the steps.

My mind full, I step toward the railing and stare into the sea. What once seemed familiar brings a cloud of uncertainty. Everything inside of me is at war. What if the blade is sending me to kill my own father for Moryana's vengeance? Why has she suddenly gone quiet?

"Speak to me," I pat the dagger's hilt.

"The answers will come on the words of the King," Harmony says in a frustrating riddle.

Annoyed, I kick the side of the boat. Wendell whistles. Turning toward him, I raise an eyebrow in question. "Yes?"

"Ye be needing to clear ye mind. Come over here and learn to handle the wheel," the pirate smiles.

With nothing better to do, I leave my station and join Wendell. He opens his arms and I stand between him and the massive steering device. The wind whips through my hair and Wendell positions my hands on the spokes.

"Aye, more magical ink has appeared it seems," Wendell trails a finger along my bare shoulder. At a side glance, I can see the whirling pattern circling my arm. Used to new branding appearing, I shrug.

"I thinks it adds to yer beauty," Wendell plants a kiss on the spot, sending a shiver through me.

"Thank you," I stare at the horizon. My gut tells me we're getting close to my father's waters. My muscles tense and I grit my teeth to gain some semblance of calm.

"I found food," Storm announces. Oli jumps down to help him. They work together to drag a few barrels and crates over, forming a table on the quarterdeck and then disappearing again to bring up the food. I watch curious as to what they scrounged up, hopeful it's palatable.

"Aye, but where's the rum?" Wendell peers at the crates the guys brought up.

"Never to worry. This is the Jolly Barnacle after all," Oli laughs as he pulls out a bottle.

Wendell leaves my side. He grabs the bottle and pulls out the cork with his teeth before taking a long draw. "Come, lass, the ship will fare fine for a while, the waters are calm." The pirate moves to my side, placing a block at the bottom of the wheel to keep it steady.

I let Wendell lead me to the makeshift table. He takes a seat and pulls me into his lap. "Here, I think you need this more than I do," he hands the amber bottle to me.

"Thanks," I take the rum with shaky hands. I am excited to see my father again but I'm not his little girl anymore. Hell, I'm not even the woman he transformed to be with the love of my life. I can't help but wonder if he will help me again? Or will he try and talk some sense into me?

I tip the bottle back and the liquid burns down my throat but I don't stop guzzling until a set of hands pull the glass from me. "I wasn't done with that," I complain.

"Save some for the rest of us," Oli jokes as he takes a sip.

"What's going on in that pretty, little head of yours?" Storm questions with his eyebrow raised.

"I just haven't talked to my father since I left the sea. He gave me the chance to be happy and now my life is a mess. My husband was murdered and I have left a trail of blood in my wake. Will he banish me or embrace me? Will he freak out at my black fin?" I question, my words spilling out in a rush.

"Take a breath. Drowning yourself in rum may not be the best thing to do before this confrontation with your father," Storm comments.

"Maybe, but it helps take the edge off," I hiccup.

That gets a laugh from my three men.

"Be that as it may, lass, you be needing a clear head to talk to him," my pirate says.

I lean back into Wendell. There's no denying that he is right, even being near to him helps.

"Will you have to go into the water to talk to King Triton?" Oli asks.

"Depends, Daddy is a demi-god after all, but he does what he wants on his terms. So, if he sees fit for an underwater chat that's what it will be. I'm sure Sebastian will tell him about my fin, so he'll want to see it for himself," I sigh.

"I just wish there was a way we could go with you. I mean I can swim but I'm no merman." Storm's shoulders sag.

"Yes, that makes me nervous as well. I don't know what my father will think when he hears that I have three new men in my life so soon after my husband's death," I mention as I take a piece of cheese from the plate in front of me.

"How long until we break his kingdom?" Oli questions.

I stand and move towards the front of the Jolly, all three men in tow, as I search the seas for the signs. Far on the horizon, I spot the purple reef just under the sea cap.

"There, do you see the little bit of purple hue? That is a sign of the start of his realm. We're nearly there," I wrap my arms around my middle. A shiver runs through my body as they squint to make out the boundary.

I turn to my pirate, "Are you sure that I can't have any more rum?"

He laughs before shaking his head no. "Aye, as much as I love me some rum, a clear head is called for in the situation. The eels are your mission, they need to be taken care of so your name will be cleared and you can start anew. With the three of us, if that is your wish."

I smile at him, just as the boat lurches to a stop. I'm thrown forward, head-first in the water, changing as the water touches my skin. No matter the reason, it's freeing to be rid of the cloth that humans wear. No doubt, I understand why they wear them, but the garments almost feel like a cage, binding me in my human skin.

I grimace at the appearance of my black scales but continue my descent to the sea floor. I relish the ease of swimming once again with my fin, I can't believe how much I have missed this. In mere minutes, I'm floating in front of the gate to my former home. The two merfolk that guard the gate raise their weapons at me.

"I am Ariel, daughter of King Triton. Sebastian should have swam ahead and informed my father I was on my way," I say, holding up my hands to show them I am unarmed.

"Our Princess Ariel has a pearly green fin, not jet black," one of the guards speaks up.

I sigh, "Just get my father, get Sebastian, they will recognize me."

The two guards move closer to each other to, most likely, discuss their options. Neither of them take their eyes off me and just as one of them goes to speak, the trumpets of my Father sound. The guards quickly break apart and rush to open the gates.

"Ari-el, my daughter," my father swims towards me with his arms wide open.

I can't stop the smile that breaks my lips as I open my arms in return and meet him. It feels like home being in his arms once more.

"My my, Sebastian told me your fin was black, but I didn't believe him. And this dagger with its vengeance mission did this?" he asks.

"It was the dagger that changed me, Father. I didn't have a choice. Eric…" I start to sob as a flash of his lifeless body surfaces in my memory. "He was murdered and I was blamed. I prayed to anyone that would listen, from my prison cell and Moryana answered my call. I have done some things I'm not proud of, but I'm on the trail of the beings behind it all."

I stop and glance at my Father's face, trying to read his expression, gauging whether he believes me or not.

"And the criminals are in my seas?" he asks with an eyebrow raised.

"That they are, it's Flotsam and Jetsam," I say flatly.

"Bring me back to your side," Harmony hisses.

"What is that light?" my father asks at the same time.

A heaviness settles in my bones as I remove my arms from my father so I can retrieve the blade which fell to the ocean floor. Nothing about this is simple. I'm lucky he's listened to my story so far without blowing a gasket. Once I have my hand on the hilt, I pull her free from the sand and hold her up to show my father, "This is the blade of Moryana, Harmony is her name."

ARI

At the mention of the Goddess's name, my father flinches. He holds his palm up, blocking his view of Harmony. "Ariel, when will you stop trusting others with your plights? Why do you never come to me?" My father's face contorts as he fights back his anger.

"Daddy, I was on land in a human jail. There was no way to come to you," I bite back a roar.

"I wish you would have listened to me and never left the safety of our waters." He turns from me and my heart sinks. As soon as Harmony is at my side again, my connection to this place dims. My emotions fade.

"How long will you hold that against me? Will you help me find the twins or should I call the Goddess again?" I raise my chin in defiance.

My father swims back and forth, arms crossed. His hair floats around him like a white cloud as I watch his face become a mask. Before the dagger, I'd tremble at his fin. Now I stand, almost bored as I wait for his answer. With or without his help, my mission must continue.

"Ariel—"

"I am Ari now. I only need you to temporarily grant my men fins and gills so that I can hunt the evil eels. It is not such a huge favor," I sigh.

"Men?" King Triton's eyes widen.

"I know you want an explanation, but I don't have time to discuss this more. Each minute I am tied to this dagger, its darkness erases my light. Will you come topside with me and grant my favor or not?"

King Triton doesn't answer with words, he simply gestures for me to lead. Clasping the dagger tightly, I swim toward the Jolly Barnacle. The guards eye me with distaste as they wait for us to pass before flanking my father. Growing more and more irritable, I push my fin to move faster.

"Aye, there you are, lass," Wendell greets me from the deck when I surface.

Before I can answer, my father joins me. He calls a wave that brings us to the edge of the ship's railing. Without looking back, I leap over the railing to join my crew. Storm stands at my left, Wendell to my right, while Oli towers behind me.

"I'm losing more and more of who I am. There's really no time to talk," I state again in the presence of witnesses. "Please, Daddy."

"Ariel," King Triton sighs, "since there is nothing I can do to remove this geis, I'll grant your wish. For three days only. When the sun sets on the third day, they had better be above water or they will perish. You are not to engage with any of the merfolk. I don't want our people sullied by this darkness. When your deed is done, send word through Sebastian. He will accompany you or there will be no favor."

"Thank you." I bow my head.

"I swear you'll be the death of me someday," the King pushes forward enough to caress my jaw. "My unruly, yet most favorite daughter." He lifts his trident with a grimace and touches each man on the forehead. "Gather your wits, and anchor this ship closer to the reef before you rush into the deep. Those you seek are in the manatee graveyards," King Triton's lips purse as he turns to me one last time before disappearing into the sea.

"Oy, you want to tell me why my forehead is stinging?" Oli taps me on the shoulder.

Knowing the next words I state are bound to cause all of them to balk, I raise Harmony's ruby to my lips. "For the next part of the journey, we have to go deep into the sea. My father has granted you fins for three days," I shrug. "Did Sebastian jump aboard yet?"

"I'm here, Ari," my old friend grouches from the deck.

"FINS?" All three men yelp.

"You've seen mine, what's the big deal?"

"Aye, lass. T'id not escape my notice that while ye were scaly, ye had no nether parts either," Wendell places a hand over his groin. "Me thinks it would be better to stay aboard the Jolly Barnacle."

"You'd leave me to finish this quest alone in favor of your man parts?" I raise an eyebrow.

Storm coughs and Wendell's cheeks redden. "Nay, I

told ya I'd follow ya anywhere, if the bottom of the sea be the place, I'll go," Wendell sighs, "Storm, help me secure the Jolly and we can head out."

"So, do we need to shed our clothes? Exactly how does this magic work?" Oli asks as the other two set to work.

"Depends on if you'd like to keep your clothes or not?" I say with a little laugh.

"How are you still dressed?" he questions. "You were just a mermaid, but you aren't naked."

"Do you really think that my father would want to see me without clothes? He used his magic to dress me as I boarded," I inform him.

"Fair enough. So, should I undress now?" he asks.

"I have no objection to that, Storm and Wendell may," I remind him.

"Maybe I'll see if they need any help," Oli states as he heads towards the other two.

I lean on the railing, enjoying the ocean view.

"Ari-el," Sebastian starts, "You sure you want to go after the eels? They are nothing but trouble."

"Yes, they are, but Harmony," I say, patting the dagger on my hip. "Points me to them, they are the ones responsible for Eric's death. I was promised vengeance and this dagger is the way that I get it. Just as I started my happily ever after, I was robbed of it. If you gave up part of who you were for love and it was cruelly taken from you, could you stand by and do nothing?"

Sebastian paces a little on the railing before he stops

and places a claw on my hand, "I just worry for you. You are right in your quest, but I wish you didn't have to go around murdering. You be a princess, your life should've been a fairytale. I am with you on this part of the mission. I'll do what I can to help you."

"Thank you, Sebastian. I'm grateful for your help," I say with a smile.

"Aye, Ari, we are ready, if you are," Wendell says as he walks up beside me.

"Let's go. Disrobe and take your weapon belts in your hands. They will fall from your waist if you wear them when you transform," I tell them as I start to strip. Taking into account the dagger, I grab the scabbard and strap it over one shoulder instead of around my waist.

There's a little splash, that tells me that Sebastian went ahead of us into the sea.

My guys disrobe and I sneak a little peek and have to stop a laugh when I notice that they are all looking straight ahead. Neither of them dare to glance at the man next to them.

"I'm ready," I announce as I grip Harmony in one hand.

"Aye," the three say at the same time.

"Let's go. It's half a day's swim to get there. We will need to find a cave to rest before we fight the twins," I inform them.

"This is going to be so strange, is breathing under water any different than on land?" Storm asks.

"Not really, the fin will be the biggest challenge for you. At least I think so. Feet were so hard for me. I was like a newborn babe on the sand. Lucky for me, I was alone and got some practice before Eric came across me," I smile at the memory of it.

"This breeze is nice on my nether regions, but a little nippy. I think it's time for a dip," Storm states, just before he jumps overboard.

I watch as the other two follow behind him directly and I join them, welcoming my fin once again.

Doing a little circle, I watch as the men experiment with their tails. I notice that all three are as different as can be. Wendell's is amber with gold flecks that shimmer in the sun's rays, whereas Oli's is that of flames—reds, oranges and yellows. Finally, my Storm, his is that of blues like the night sky with flecks of silver as if he was painted with the stars.

"If you three are ready, follow me," Sebastian says.

"Aye, lead the way," Wendell swims up next to me.

"You go ahead, I'm gonna hang in the back until you three get used to your fins," I gesture with a grin.

"If ye want to see how me ass looks as a merman, ye only have to ask," he smirks as he swims after Sebastian.

Oli and Storm follow and I bring up the rear. I don't only admire my men as they flip and kick their fins, but also the beauty of the sea that surrounds us. This moment makes me wish there was a way to live in both worlds, but I made my choice.

"Ari-el, get your head back into the ocean. We have a long journey ahead," Sebastian calls, bringing me back from my thoughts.

"Why don't you sing us a tune?" I ask.

"Me? You're the one with the voice, why don't you bless us with something?" he counters.

"My song is what activates the dagger, best save it for when we need to fight," I reply.

"Fine," he says before he starts his song.

We have been traveling for a few hours, when I call for a break. Each of the guys have done better with their fins than I did with legs, but they're definitely ready to rest.

Sebastian descends to the ocean floor, finding a spot with enough coral to hide among. The guys and I follow him, tucking into an alcove surrounded by kelp. The three seem right at home as they settle in the sand.

"I don't think we'll find a better hiding place," Sebastian clicks his claw as he paces. "I don't like being this exposed but I doubt we will find a sea cave here that is empty. We're far from the zone of safety, this is shark territory."

"What if we weave the kelp together on this side?" I point to the biggest opening. The coral forms a triangle behind us, leaving us open to the water where the kelp thins.

"Maybe two of us could go scout to see if we can find a deeper cave?" Storm asks, his face scrunched with worry.

"Excuse me?" a tiny voice calls from the ocean floor.

Startled, I dip behind a huge, green leaf. Searching

for the owner of the voice, I scan around until I see a purple seahorse clinging to the very branch I'm holding. "Hello," the seahorse waves a fin. "I know where you can find a good hiding place, I'll show you if you take me with you. I seem to have lost my family."

Raising an eyebrow, I look over to Sebastian. He gestures for me to pick him up, so I bring him to the seahorse's level. "Whatchoo doing on this side of the reef?" Sebastian's left eye pops wide open.

"I got caught in a net, but there was a hole and I escaped," he says in a rush. "I've been watching and listening from this kelp bed, but it's too risky to cross the open water alone."

"Okay, we will help you. What should we call you?" I ask.

"Benny," the little guy smiles.

"Well, Benny, climb on," I put a finger in front of him and he wraps his tail around the digit.

"We haven't been underwater for an hour and my brain is full," Storm stares at Benny. "Lead on, little horse."

With Benny's directions, we head across the chasm and find a nice cave to use for the night. Just before we get there he squeals as a stingray glides by calling his name. Apparently, his family sent the ray to find him. He clutches onto the side of his savior and they swim away. Relieved to have helped, I search the cave for a soft spot to lay.

"Everyone, bed down. We have a long journey ahead in the morning." I pat the sand beside me. The guys look back and forth between them before joining me. Storm curls up on one side of me with Oli on the other. Wendell settles for a spot on a ledge above us. Sebastian grumbles before circling into a spot. The next thing I know, my eyes grow heavy.

WENDELL

Waking up as a merman is an odd sensation. It took me a moment of pure panic as I sank toward the ocean floor until I remembered that I had a fin.

"Wendell, ye idiot," I mutter to myself.

Abashed, I focus on the flipper and wiggle it. Although in me mind, it is like giving a wee kick. The action causes me to rise, so I do it again. It's freeing and weird all at the same time. The worst part of it all is when I glance down. Me heart does a tumble when I remember me missing member, but I tell myself that it's still there under the scales. I've no heart to actually check, blimey.

"Looks like you need to reacclimate." Ari notices my antics with a giggle. "Let's swim around a little bit before we head off, but we need to leave soon. Three days in this form may not be long enough to find the twins," Ari reminds us.

Oli and Storm join me as I engage in some more testing of me swimming. Before long, we have the hang of it enough that Ari says we are ready to leave. I've always loved the ocean, but being under the waves I usually navigate is a whole new world for me.

I can't stop staring at the fish pods swimming past us. Not much seems to spook them. One even came close enough to me that I could reach out and touch it. I tried, but was too slow. Aye, I swear it was giving me a dirty look as it swam away. Is that even possible?

We swam for what seemed like days until Ari said it was break time. I knew that it was mere hours but I was already sore. Some sidekick I'm turning out to be, nothing more than a yellow-belly. If I already hurt like this, how will I last the rest of the trip? I rested on a nice piece of coral that was softer than I would expect it to be.

"Aye, how are you two faring with yer tails?" I ask, giving mine a little flip.

"Now that I've got the hang of it, it's not so bad," Oli comments.

"It's definitely different than walking; but a welcome change. I was never the strongest swimmer," Storm says.

"Aye, I thinks I have fallen in love with the sea once again, but differently. It be a wonderful sight to see it from this side," I tell them.

Ari smiles, "I'm glad to hear that. It's time to leave. I've got another helper to lead the way," she holds up her finger showing another tiny seahorse. After all the odd things that have happened since Ari walked into my life, there's no reason to object or question her now.

The manatee graveyards are a place that no fish ever wishes to visit. The trench is long, dark, and full of death. Every malicious sea creature flocks to its shadows. Even the water seems ill. My team and I approach the barrier of kelp that acts as a hunting ground before the trench carefully. We've had plenty of time to think up a plan, but since none of us have been here before—it is all moot.

"This seems like a bad idea," Oli slashes his sword through the water, testing his strength below.

"Aye, none of us are at peak performance besides ye, lass," I agree. Although I think t'was a better choice to carry my two daggers instead of a sword. Testing them, I nod to myself.

Ari lets out a long sigh. "We don't have a choice. Now that the twins know we're on to them, there's no way they'll come topside. We've got Harmony on our side and the Goddess. Stop worrying so much." I bite back a retort as I'm also feeling out of my league but the desire to press on is too strong.

Leaning against a huge rock, Ari's face changes like the tides.

"A copper for yer thoughts?" I tap her shoulder.

"Ah, I was just pondering the course of my life since receiving the dagger. Moryana said it would change me, but, honestly, I'm surprised. There is a strong urge within me to kill those responsible for Eric's death, and I didn't hesitate to carry out murder in the Goddess's name without question. But otherwise? I'm still me, right?"

"Ari?" Sebastian clicks his claw. "Get yo head in the game, little mermaid. This is no time for daydreamin'! Of course, you're still yourself, who else might you be?"

Shaking herself out of the daze, Ari's face settles

into one of pure determination. I nod, staring at the course ahead. There's no clear route through the graveyard and I'm hesitant to swim right into the thick of it.

"Let's scout around this barrier of kelp first," I suggest. "I'd like to get a better idea of what fresh hell we're about to enter."

"That sure sounds better than the alternative," Storm replies. "My tracking skills aren't much use down here."

"Young man, open your eyes," Sebastian waves his claws. "Even sea creatures leave a mark when they travel. Dig deep within yourself and you'll find you have the skills no matter your location."

Storm stares at the little crab for a moment and then his face lights up as the advice registers. "I'll take the lead, let's follow the current...this way." He points toward the left. I haven't got the heart to tell him that we've eventually got to dive into the trench that follows the barrier.

Storm and Oli lead the group as we zigzag through the thick kelp bed. In what should be a lush feeding ground, we find no signs of life at all. A coldness seeps into me bones as we press onward, closer and closer to the trench.

"Blimey, those sea walls are high. Are we headed there?" I point to the entrance. The two rocky sea walls are about ten feet apart and as high as the tallest trees on land. A few sea plants cling to an alcove here and there, but our view is mostly gray stone and dark, murky water.

"I'm afraid so," Ari grips Harmony and holds her in

SINGING DAGGER

front of her body. The ruby glows, but the dagger is silent from what I can tell.

"Stick close to the sides," Oli motions to the wall. "Those eels could be hiding in any nook or cranny."

Clenching my teeth. I follow Ari. She scoops the little crab up and places him on her shoulder. I wish I'd have thought to bring a bag to hide him, but maybe it's best for him to be able to scramble away if things get crazy.

We travel along the side of the trench for what feels like an hour, but is probably more like twenty minutes before the walls widen enough that a ship could pass through. The further we get, the less we're able to see.

"Slow down, there's something up there," Storm points to something glowing beyond the next bend.

Me heart thumps so loudly it's a wonder no one remarks about it, but I take a breath and press forward. When we reach the edge of the wall, Storm peeks around. His head disappears before he jerks back to his position.

"This is bad." He gulps.

Shoving my way past him, I take a turn looking. At first, I can't see anything as my eyes adjust. Once they do, my mouth falls open. Mere feet away from me the Goddess lays inside a giant clam. Whispering into each ear are none other than the two slimy eels.

Ari pushes past me, dagger in the air. I try to grab her but it's no use.

"Explain this to me!" she growls, snatching one of the eels from her side and pressing the blade against its gills.

"Don't you dare hurt my poopsy," Moryana hisses.

There is a spark of electricity from the eel she holds, causing me to yip in pain, but she doesn't release him.

"I should gut you just for that," Ari yells at the eel, then turns back to the Goddess. "Why would you do this to me? Kill my husband? Send me on a quest of vengeance just to lead me back to yourself?"

"You really are daft, aren't you?" the woman asks as her body begins to shift and change.

Still clutching the eel, Ari moves back. Storm and I lurch forward, preparing for a fight.

"Give me my baby back," the bitch cries as she sprouts tentacles where her feet were. To my horror, the beautiful lady transforms into a large half-lady, half-black octopus. Clenching my daggers, I push toward Ari.

"It's the sea witch that took my voice and tried to take a hell of a lot more than that from me," our lass gasps. "How? Eric killed you. There is no way you could've survived that." She turns white.

"You aren't the only one that can strike a bargain with a Goddess, dear," Ursula smirks at me.

"Blood," Harmony demands. *"Kill all three."*

For the first time, we can all hear the blade.

"Give me back my baby and I may just let you leave here unharmed," the sea witch gloats.

"It's you who should be afraid," Ari grits as she guts the eel in one swift motion. I want to help, but my body is frozen in shock.

The witch wails in anger, lurching forward to

attack, but Oli and Storm cut her off, acting as Ari's shield.

"How's it feel to lose someone you love?" Ari taunts, waving the limp eel above her head before letting loose. He sinks to the seafloor, kicking up a little sand in his wake.

The other twin starts to arc, sparks flying from his slimy body as he swims toward us.

"I crave blood, the witch is mine," Harmony whispers.

"I get the witch," Ari claims, swimming around the two men and toward the monster.

Ursula scans the area for a weapon, but I don't give her the chance to grab anything as I swim between her and Ari, slashing with my daggers. I score a hit on the arm that she brought up at the last minute to protect her heart. Seizing the moment, Ari slides in with Harmony and plunges the blade to the hilt. Harmony hisses with pleasure as black goo drips from her blade.

"You bitch, do you really think that you can kill me?" Ursula shrieks, trying to back away.

"You killed my husband, your life is forfeit. The Goddess promised me vengeance and I will take it!" Ari shrieks, raising the blade once more.

This gets a laugh from the Sea Witch, "How is she any different then me? I gave you the potion that gave you legs. Without me, you never would have been with the prince."

"He is dead, did you forget that? You killed him and framed me. Why?" the princess demands.

"You tried to kill me and my babies. Lucky for us, I had a plan in place. I was never dead, only dormant. It took time to regain my strength and that gave me a little time to plot my revenge," the witch boasts.

"Did you forget that you started it? I came to you for help, to be with my love and you schemed to take him from me so you could use me to get my father's kingdom. Any of that ringing a bell? And you killed him, for what? Did you think that I would just roll over and die with him? You didn't gain anything by murdering him, other then a death sentence." Ari seems genuinely confused.

A mask falls over Ari's face and she moves forward, slicing with the blade again. Ursula screams as the blade sinks into her heart. There is a look of surprise on her face as Ari removes Harmony. With a wail, she crumbles to the sea floor.

Moving forward, I pin the witch to the ground with my blades. The little crab jumps down to check that the witch is really dead this time. He nods his little head in confirmation. "There is no life to the witch now as far as I can tell. Can you ask the blade?"

Storm and Oli swim over with the second limp eel.

"Took you long enough," I tease.

"He was a slippery bugger," Oli shrugs.

Storm joins me at the witch's body and in one swift motion, takes off her head.

"She was dead already," I sigh.

"Well, now there is no debate on that," he smiles at me.

"Thank you," Ari's eyes glaze over as she stares into the red ruby at Harmony's grip. "It is over, she whispers. "Where to now? Are we to return you to the Goddess?"

The blade vibrates and hums before spinning back toward the direction from whence we came. An image of King Triton floats in front of us. "What? Why am I going back to King Triton? We found the murderers and took care of them," Ari states in disbelief.

"You promised to fulfill revenge for Moryana, this is her command. Go back to Atlantica," Harmony shrills.

"What?" I ask, noticing the tears that are spilling down Ari's cheeks.

"We have to go back to my father's kingdom to finish revenge for Moryana," the lass bites out.

"What? Why?" Oli demands.

"Because, once more, I made a deal with someone without knowing all the details," Ari sniffles. "You would think that after the mess with Ursula, I wouldn't be so eager to sign up with a powerful being, but here I am again."

Ari swims away from us, leaving even the crab with its mouth open. The blade can't mean to have her kill her father—can it?

"Well, don't just watch her, pick me up and let's go!" Sebastian screams.

Oli and I exchange a look before I scoop up Sebastian and swim after our princess.

ARI

My heart races as I swim away from my men. I can't let them see how a part of me in fact wants to kill my father. I'm tired of being caught up by those who wish to destroy him, like a pawn on a chessboard. Maybe it's better to just let him go?

"It is your destiny," the glow from Harmony turns the water red around me.

Harmony heats my palm and my blood runs cold. The waters around me dim and I can almost feel my heart harden. Not daring to look back, I swim toward Atlantica at top speed. There's no way the three fin rookies behind me will be able to keep up.

"Vengeance," I hiss as I exit the trench and speed through the open water.

Images flash through my mind of every time King Triton has yelled at me—of which there are many. His face, a mask of anger fuels me forward. Rage builds inside of me until my insides feel as if they might explode. I'd do anything to release this energy.

The pull of the dagger is strong. The closer I get to

King Triton, the hotter the blade becomes. Instinctively, I know that even if I tried to drop Harmony, I could not. We are one.

Nothing about the seascape registers in my mind. All I know is that I need to keep moving. I have no plan, just an outcome in mind. King Triton must fall. A tickle in the back of my mind threatens to stop me, but I push the thought back. There's nothing that can remove the death sentence and I must be the one to carry it out.

A familiar rock formation stops me momentarily. What's left of my treasure cave from long ago now lay in ruins. My throat burns as I recall that day, how the King blasted everything I held dear with the flick of his trident. The red glow brightens and I set a course for the castle.

Merfolk swim here and there, none daring to cast their gaze upon me. No matter, they are inconsequential. Crossing through the courtyard, I approach the castle entrance. My hand clenches Harmony. Taking a deep breath, I swim forward.

"Excuse me," a guard lowers a spear in front of me. "The palace is shut down. King Triton is not to be disturbed."

"I will not disturb him," I blink. "I simply wish to visit my room and check on my sisters. Don't you remember me? I'm the youngest daughter of the King."

"I'm sorry, miss, I don't recognize you. I'll have to ask you to leave.

Without a thought, I break past him, leading him into a dead-end hall. He shouts and swims after me, which was my intent. As soon as we're out of sight, I turn swiftly and slice his throat open, from gill to gill. The guard's eyes open wide, but no sound escapes as he drops to the ground. As quickly as possible I drag him behind a statue of a long lost Goddess and dart toward the King's chamber.

"Blood," Harmony demands, her voice so loud it hurts my head.

"Soon, I have to take care not to get caught. If anyone finds me, they'll throw me into the palace prison. If that happens, I will never get what you want," I remind her.

She simmers down, but not completely. Tucking the hilt under my arm, I grimace. The red glow is too bright for comfort. "You need to turn off that light," I hiss. The blade trembles and dims enough that red doesn't surround me.

The King's chambers are the last ones, of course. Sneaking from statue to statue, I make slow progress through the hall. Lucky for me, there's no one out and about. There must have been orders for everyone to clear the space, even the servants.

Taking advantage of the quiet, I cross the last portion of the palace quickly and stop just short of the huge double doors that will lead me to Triton. Nothing that makes me exist anymore, only the mission. My vision goes red as I reach for the handle and pull. Inside of the room, Triton faces his shellshelf with his back to me. Wasting no time, I cross the room and raise the dagger high. A moment before impact, he turns and grabs my wrist.

"Ah, it's as I guessed. The Goddess has put you under her geis," Triton brings his bearded face to mine. "Ariel? Can you hear me?"

My heart thumps. With all my might, I try to break free of his grasp, but it's no use. "My. Name. Is. Ari. And you must die!" I yell.

The King's face crumples. His grip tightens and he drags me across the room to a large, golden stand. From the stand, he grabs his trident and raises it toward the blade in my hand. A white light envelops me, but it's soon overpowered by red.

"It is no use," Harmony sings. *"Bend the fin and take your death cleanly!"*

"Ariel, my ever-changing child. Why must every evil thing try to use you against me?" His lips turn downward. "I hope you do not remember this moment," Triton sighs as he brings both of our hands down toward his chest rapidly. The blade pierces his chest and lodges in his heart. Our eyes meet and then he falls to the ground with the rubied hilt sticking out of his body. Blood leaks out, creating a darker-red tinge to the glowing water.

"Ari? What have you done?" a voice cries from behind me.

All at once, the world flip-flops. The hatred and heat seep out of my body, leaving me cold and barren. Whipping around frantically, I search for the voice. My gaze stops on a small blue-and-yellow fish with three mermen behind it.

"Ari?" I place a palm on my forehead as a sharp pain doubles me over. Retching on the smooth floor, I try to steady myself. Hands clasp at my shoulders and I look up into a set of blue eyes.

"Ari, we have to get out of here. You've killed the king. All in the kingdom will be out for your head!" The merman tugs me toward the door. Something tickles at the back of my mind, but I don't have the energy to pursue the thought. The three mermen lead me out of a window and race across the water with me. They don't stop until we come to a small cave. Once inside, one of them covers the opening with a large boulder.

"Lass? Have ye lost yer mind?" the darker one asks.

"I, uh, I don't know what you're talking about," I whisper as a maelstrom of memories smash through my consciousness.

"T'was that damned blade," he growls. "Give it to me, Oli."

"Are you sure, Wendell?" the other asks while swimming toward us.

Before I can speak, or make sense of what my memories are telling me, Oli hands Wendell a dagger. The merman takes the closest rock and smashes the giant ruby at the blade's hilt, cracking it.

"Who are you? Why have the three of you taken me from my home? I didn't kill the king. He is my father," my words are a little bit of a jumble but my brain is screaming for me to get away from these merman.

"Ari, it's us," the one closest to me replies.

"I don't know you," I state, recoiling as he moves nearer to me.

"How did I get a black fin? This can't be good, I

need to surface before whatever spell I'm under is undone." I begin to panic as I dart toward the exit of the cave, pushing the rock to the side.

"Wait for us!" one of the strange mermen yells at me.

But I don't, there is nothing good about me having no memory of these males or how I have a tail again. A deep ache gnaws at my insides, I long to get back to my husband and my life on land. A flash of pain sears my temples as a flash of memory hits me. Eric's lifeless body floods my mind. All the blood. No!

"Oh, Eric," I whisper. Panic sets in and I begin swimming and rack my brain as to how I got into the ocean in the first place.

My fin carries me swift toward the surface as if I had never exchanged it for legs. At this moment, I'm grateful, because those legs would be useless as I have never learned to swim with them.

The crown of my head emerges from the water just as I notice that tingle of magic changing me back to human. A wave of hopelessness threatens to sink me as the realization hits me that I'm stranded in the middle of the sea.

The three mermen surface near me as I start to go back under. Terrified that I might drown, I wave my hands and kick my feet to try and stay afloat. I open my mouth to scream for help when a wave crashes into my mouth and all I taste is the salt of the sea. I refuse to give up, even though I'm slowly sinking back to the ocean floor. Thanks to the gods, a strong pair of arms wraps around me. They hold tight as we travel back to the surface.

"Lass, what are ye doing? Trying to drown yerself will not get rid of the three of us that easily," he jokes.

"What? No, I can't swim in human form. I never learned," I confess.

"Aye, ain't that always the way?" He winks and something stirs in the back of my mind. Fragments of memory flash through my mind. One image in particular brings heat to my cheeks; Wendell's face as he hovers above me with naught but the night draped over his skin. "Oh," I breathe as I scan the other two faces hoping to jog more memories. The only thing I can squeeze out of my brain are the names of the other two men. There's a familiarity about them that I'll need to get straight but for now, we need to find land.

"Just a few more strokes," Storm calls from his spot at our side.

Looking over, I spot a large pirate ship. The Kraken at the hull spears my head with another memory. I remember sitting on the deck playing cards with the men. One by one, every moment since I woke up in the jail washes over me. My heart clenches at the quest I brought these men on. When the last of the images ends, I almost break in half. Father! How could I have done such a thing?

"Hold on there, Lass, I've got you." Wendell holds me tighter.

Before we can grab the rope ladder, the water begins to churn, spinning us in a circle. A throne made of two giant clams rises with Moryana sitting in the seat, wielding my father's trident.

"Did you think you'd get rid of me so easily, little mermaid?" She chuckles.

It makes my blood run cold, I'm such an idiot, of course, it was the Goddess this whole time.

"It was you, wasn't it? You set this all in motion? Why? You had my husband killed and after all the wild goose chase you set me on—your intent was for me to kill my father."

There's nothing I'd like better than to tear her apart, piece by piece and feed her to the fishes.

"You were a means to an end. The end of Triton's rule over the seas," she states with a wicked grin.

How can I defeat a Goddess? I'm weaponless, the blade she gifted me lay at the sea floor where Wendell smashed the ruby. The men are naked just as I am, but at least they have their blades strapped to their chests.

"Whatever you're thinking, Ari. It's not going to work. Many have tried to kill me only to perish. Strangely enough, I don't want you to die. Seeing that I got what I wanted—to rule the sea, I'd like to offer you the rule of Tirulia in my stead. For your loyalty, I'll dampen the ugly memories you carry with you. It will be simple enough to smooth the Eric thing over and you will be their princess once more. I'll even let you keep these three by your side if you so wish," Moryana says as she runs an eye over each one.

Under her gaze, the men realize that they are nude and try to hide their members from the Goddess. It's cute, really.

"You think I'm so heartless I'd forget killing my own father? Besides, the twins are dead, who will you pin the death on? The town will not just forget that I was found covered in Eric's blood," I state, placing my hands on my hips.

"You let me worry about the details. You can have your happily ever after with these men. But if you make a move against me, the penalty will be death. First, I'll kill each of them slowly as you watch before it is your turn. I am the Goddess of Vengeance, after all," she says with a smirk. "So, what is your choice, rule or death?"

It wasn't really a hard choice, as much as I longed to kill her, rule was the only option.

"Is there really a choice? Rule, it is." I sigh.

She gives me a little nod, "Stay on this ship until my return. Once I do, land will be yours." With that, Moryana disappears in a cloud of smoke, leaving us standing on the deck of the pirate ship, unsure of what is next.

"I don't know about you lackeys, but I best gather me clothes. I don't mind Ari being naked as a jaybird, but me willy hasn't seen the light of day for years," Wendell says as he heads towards his quarters.

I follow him, because he is right, the last thing we need on top of all of this is a sunburn.

Oli scoops me up before I make it over the threshold. "You okay, Ari?" he asks, as he sets me on the bed. His eyes almost pierce me with their tenderness.

Swallowing back the lump in my throat, I shake my head. "No, but I will be. Even now, my memories of before the jail are faint. I'm sorry I dragged you all into this." I bite back tears. "In the end, my father buried the blade in his own heart for me. There's nothing the Goddess could do that will erase that," I stop, my lip quivering.

"Oh, Ari," Oli pulls me to his chest, "I wish we could have caught up with you faster."

"You don't hate me for what I've done?" The sob I hold in bursts forth.

"Never," Wendell steps to my side, smoothing back the mess of hair that's flopped into my face.

"We told you once, but I'll tell you every day if I have to," Oli lifts my chin. "We belong to you."

"That's right," Storm puts a hand on my shoulder. "Maybe there's still some way to salvage our situation with the Goddess as well."

Relief washes over me. I've never felt so understood, even with my late husband. "I thought you might leave me."

"I think that ship has sailed, Lass," Wendell laughs.

"Har, har. Keep it up and you'll be sleeping on deck tonight," I joke with a smile.

"How long until Moryana is back?" Storm asks, moving a little closer to me.

"Hours? Days?" Who can know?" I reply with a yawn, "But for now, I think a nap is in order. Since all of this began I've not had a proper night's sleep. Nightmares be damned, I'm tired."

I scoot back on the bed and Storm and Oli slide into the sheets with me. Wendell leans down for a peck and then finishes dressing.

"If ye need me, I be manning the wheel," he says as he heads for the door.

"I'll always need you," I say as he turns for one last glance, a smile on his lips as he exits the quarters.

With two of the three of my men around me, I relax enough to fall into a deep sleep for the first time in a long time.

ARI

The sound of a seagull squawking wakes me. Burying my head in the blankets, I push Storm out of the bed. "Go see what's happening. I can't bear to see any of the creatures from my past life."

Storm's eyebrows raise. "Are you sure?"

Nodding slowly I bite my lip. "I'm sure. If I'm going to live this life, I have to break ties with anything that ties me to the sea. Once Moryana returns, we're headed to land and I'll never come near Atlantica again."

"As you wish," Storm bows before dragging on pants. Watching him wriggle his firm buttocks into the material makes me yearn for more time in bed.

Snuggling into Oli's side, I listen to the commotion. Oli's arms wrap around my middle and he places a kiss on my cheek. "Did you sleep well?"

Smiling, I realize I did. For once, there were no nightmares. Taking a deep breath, I close my eyes and seek inward. Nothing. The grief is gone, along with most of my memories that don't include Storm, Wendell, and Oli. Everything from my past has been reduced to a kaleidoscope of colors. What's weird is I know who I was, it just all feels like it was a story I read.

"I slept fine," I whisper. "I just want to get back to land and start our new life. Everything about this makes me nervous. Why did I agree to work with her?"

"To save all our lives," Oli says simply. "I don't think you had a choice, my love."

My cheeks flare at the 'L' word, but I keep my cool. Too bad Moryana didn't banish us to some tropical island. Now that I could get behind. I can't quite pin my finger on it, but her having me rule Tirulia in her stead has to be bigger than I can see. Otherwise, she could place any one of her minions on the throne—assuming she has droves.

"That bird is stubborn," Storm reappears. "He refuses to leave unless you tell him yourself."

Blowing a stray strand of hair from my face, I sigh. "Fine. Is there a gown I can throw on?"

"Aye," Wendell peeks in the door. "Rummage through the chest under the window. Hurry before this sea chicken plasters me deck in white."

Storm laughs as he crosses the cabin and opens the chest. After a moment of digging, he pulls out a black gown with a matching sheer shawl. Opening my hands, I wait for the clothing. The material slips over my head easily, hugging my frame with its softness. Wrapping the shawl over one shoulder, I head toward the deck.

"You wish to see me?" I step up to the railing and peer at Scuttle. The bird tilts his head to the side, judging my appearance or maybe my sanity.

"Kid, you've got to come back to Atlantica," he

paces. "The King is dead, and your sisters are being held captive by a crazy sea Goddess." Feathers fly into the air as he waves his wings about.

"I know." My throat dries. "Moryana is now the queen of Atlantica. There's nothing I can do." I turn away from the bird. I should feel devastated right now, but I only long for Harmony to be back in my palm.

"We are one."

"Moryana?" Reality hits scuttle and he backs away from me. "Kid? Please tell me you weren't involved in this!"

"Go away, Scuttle. I'm no longer the little mermaid you once knew. I am Ari and I will be queen of Tirulia. If you value your life, never come back to me again. Tell Sebastian and Flounder the same." I shoo him off the rail.

The seagull squawks, but flies away without another word. I watch him disappear, dry eyed. My heart is closed to anything of the past. There's only room for tomorrow. Taking a deep breath, I turn toward Wendell.

"Do we have anything to eat? I'm famished."

"Nay, but I've got fishing gear?" He winces.

"That'll do," I nod before turning away. "I've got to find your bathroom, then I'll help catch lunch."

"'Tis the bucket in my chambers," my pirate says.

"Lovely," I say with a sour look on my face. My days as a pirate are almost over, I remind myself.

I head back and eye the brass bucket that Wendell uses as a bathroom and I almost turn around. But then holding it is not an option, either.

It takes me longer to hike up my gown than to relieve myself. I'm at the washing basin when I hear Oli calling my name.

"I'll be out in a moment," I answer while cleaning my hands.

As I search for something to dry my hands with, the door flings open. I jump back, not sure what to expect. Storm pokes his head in and informs me I have some more visitors. Sighing, I shake my hands in the air before patting them on my gown and heading back out on the deck.

"Ari-el," Sebastian says as the sunlight blinds me.

"I told Scuttle to tell you to leave me be," I state, irritation in my tone.

"Why would you tell him that?" Sebastian asks.

"I'm washing my hands of the ocean and my former life," I say flatly.

"Say it ain't so," the crab shakes his head. "Here I have come with word that your father has been killed and you no longer care? What happened to you?"

"A path has been chosen for me. There is no room for the ocean in it any more. I will be Princess Ari of Tirulia from here on out. Leave me be, I beg you. Swim off and be gone," I say, doing my best to keep the tears at bay. I will not let anyone see me cry, again. Turning away, I head toward the wheel, when there is a splash behind me, I know that Sebastian is gone.

"Lass, are ye sure that's what ye want?" Wendell asks, hooking two fingers under my chin, lifting it so I'm looking him in the eyes.

"Aye, I am a mermaid no more. I choose love and

life on land, not heartache and grief below the water," I reply, my eyes never wavering from his.

"As you wish, Lass," he says, with a sad smile.

There is a boom on deck, startling Wendell and me, we turn to find Moryana has returned.

Oli and Storm move from where they were on the boat to come stand behind me.

"So, Princess, are you ready to go back to your home?" she asks with a smirk.

"You've cleared everything up already?" I ask in disbelief.

"Do you forget that I'm a Goddess? It doesn't take long for me to do mundane human things. The jailer that wasn't kind to you after Eric's death will be executed in the morning. Seems that he was caught stealing from the royal family and ended when the Prince walked in on him, he stabbed him. You walked in just after and tried to save your husband but he knocked you out cold. The king has agreed that you are to remain the crowned princess of Tirulia. See, I keep my word, will you do the same?" Moryana asks.

"Aye," is all I say with a little nod.

"Then start your journey back to land, if any of the humans try to rise up against you, use this to call me. I will make it right," the Goddess says as she holds Harmony out towards me.

"If I take this once more, will I be under a trance? Same as last time?" I ask, even as my palm itches to hold the blade.

"This time, Harmony is yours to command, but she

will be linked to me if the need arises that you need my help," she informs me.

Before I take a step toward her, I glance at each of my men and they give me a nod of their approval. Not that I need it, but we are in this together and I will not keep any secrets from them this go round. With a deep breath, I close the space between Harmony and me. Moryana places it in my hand lightly. Harmony's ruby glows and as her blade warms, a familiar and almost calming effect radiates out.

"As I said before, just sing to her if you need me and I will come," Moryana promises before she disappears in a fog of smoke.

I turn back toward my men. "Wendell, man the wheel and set sail for home."

"Aye, aye, but don't forget I be the captain," he says with a wink. "Oli, hoist the anchor and we be on our way."

Oli gets to work as Storm comes to stand next to me. "On to our next adventure, Princess."

With Wendell at the wheel, there's nothing for me to do but watch the sea. The waters churn below us roughly, as if Atlantica doesn't want us to leave. My chest tightens, as the sun hits the never ending wash of whitecaps.

Storm steps to my side, our arms touching. Without saying a word, I know he's checking on my mood. I appreciate the sentiment, but I'm fine—the Goddess has seen to that by erasing my pain. Although, in its place is a vast nothingness that will take some time to get used to, I suppose.

SINGING DAGGER

"Ari, do you see that?" Oli runs toward the rail, pointing.

Curious, I follow his aim. My mouth gapes open when I see a wave pushing a giant clam toward the ship. What now? The sea rolls toward the ship, hindering any forward progress as the clam nears. Before our eyes the waters rise and the clam is dumped on deck. Without a doubt, it's a message—from who is the question.

"Well, open up," I bend down and knock on the shell. The clam widens slowly revealing a scroll. I snatch it quickly, one never knows how long a clam will take before snapping shut again. Holding the paper to my chest, I motion toward the clam.

"Oli, put her back in the sea before she dries out," I command as I unroll the scroll and read it out loud, "Only now that vengeance can be called upon her, can the Goddess Moryana be defeated. In your possession lay the weapon to which she is vulnerable. Aim true to the heart and you will free the sea, sending the Goddess back to the realm in which she belongs."

My throat tightens as I look up. Who sent this? What will happen if I complete this quest?

"Oi, looks like ye have a choice to make, lass," Wendell wraps his arms around me from behind. "Ye fate be in yer hands again—nay anyone else's."

"What if it's a trick? There's no signature," I purse my lips. "If I make a move on Moryana and it fails—we all die."

"If you don't, what fate are you leaving your

kingdom to?" Storm asks. "We're behind you whatever you choose, but make sure you weigh your options."

Nodding, I step away and head to the captain's cabin. Storm is right, I need to think about my next move carefully. Before I can do that, I'm going to need a drink. Walking into the expansive room, I head straight for Wendell's liquor cabinet. Pulling out a dusty bottle, I bite the cork free and take a long drink. The liquid burns at first, but then leaves me calm. Settling the bottle on the table, I pace the room.

"I wish there was a way for me to see what's going on in Atlantica. Surely, the Goddess isn't a tyrant as Ursula would have been, right?" My voice echoes in the space. "Could I live with myself if I found out my sisters were being mistreated? Or my other friends? Sure, I can't feel the pain, but my conscious mind still knows where I came from."

"Sorry to intrude," Oli dips his head as he opens the cabin door. "I was elected to check on you."

"It's fine. I'm just trying to sort out this mess in my mind." I throw myself backward onto the mattress.

Oli slides into the bed next to me, his head propped on one arm. "Seems to me you know where your heart is pointing, even though it might be risky."

He's not wrong. The thing that's hanging me up is—my men. I'd risk my life in a heartbeat, but theirs? My eyes pool with water just thinking about it. "Yes, but I can't lose you," I croak.

"No matter where you go, we'll be with you," Oli's eyes seem to look right into my soul.

Turning my head, I blow out a mouthful of air. "You

can't promise that. Not when the divine are involved. So far, my track record with magical beings is pretty lame."

"But your track record with your heart is perfect," Oli nudges me before placing a kiss on my cheek.

A feeling of calm washes over me as I turn toward him. As short as our time may be, these men have been my compass. Wrapping a leg around him, I pull him closer until our lips meet. The perfect softness of his kiss warms me from my mouth to my core.

"Then it is settled. We'll sail to shore and slay a Goddess," I whisper. "But for now, I want all of you in this bed—now. Go get the others."

Oli smoothes my hair before he leaves the bed in a rush. I lay against the pillows, a single tear running down my cheek. The sound of them chattering brings a smile to my face and I quickly undress before slipping beneath the covers as I wait.

ARI

The moments I share with my men are too few to count. Before we know it, land is in sight. The castle where I spent the last year with Eric looms like a white beacon reminding me of my possible final quest. Standing at the bow, I search for a glimpse of Moryana.

A great crowd is gathered at the dock as we pull into the last open slip. When the sea of humans splits, Moryana walks down the center toward the Jolly Barnacle.

'And so there will be an audience to her demise,' I think as I touch the ruby hilt at my side.

Oli and Storm lower the plank as Wendell ties up the ship. His crew greets him below, helping with tethering her to the dock. Swallowing back the fear that threatens, I hold my head high and force a smile.

"Goddess, we thank you for such a warm welcome." I curtsy as she walks up the plank toward me.

"A welcome befitting the princess of Tirulia." Moryana waves to the crowd, and they cheer.

SINGING DAGGER

While her back is to me, I unsheathe the dagger. I have only moments to act. As Moryana turns back toward me, I begin humming as I step into her body and drive the blade deep into Moryana's chest. At first, she clutches my shoulder, eyes wide with confusion. Then her nails pierce holes in my arm as she falls to the floor: Harmony's ruby bursts, a cloud of red dust filling the air. Coughing, I wrench myself free of the Goddess's clutches.

The crowd below whispers like a hive of angry bees. They cannot see what has transpired from their angle, only that the Goddess has fallen.

"How dare you turn my weapon against me!" Moryana chokes as blood fills her mouth. "Why? I could have made you such a powerful queen!"

"You've cost this world too much already," I look down at her. "Go back to Olympus or wherever one such as you resides."

With that, the Goddess dissipates, leaving only the jewel from Harmony's hilt behind. Only now, the color is as deep as the sea. Bending down, I pick it up and hold it in my palm. My knees buckle, and I drop to the ground. The pain Moryana had veiled crashes down on me all at once, and I lose my breath.

"Ari?" Storm taps my shoulder.

Gathering myself, I look up to see a large waterspout forming beside the ship. The townspeople gasp, moving back but not leaving. A familiar figure forms within the water, and I choke back tears.

"Daddy," I run to the edge of the ship. "But I ...."

"Ariel," King Triton palms my cheek. "I'm sorry to have tricked you; it was the only way to get rid of the Goddess. The form you stabbed was naught but a golem I infused with my likeness so that vengeance could be called upon Moryana. You had to believe it for the blade to work. I hope you can forgive me."

"If you can forgive my mistake, I can forgive yours," I whisper.

"It is done." My father opens his arms in invitation, and I fall into his hold. He turns to the now chattering crowd, holding his hand up for silence.

"People of Tirulia, I am King Triton. The Goddess who walked among you has wrought the evil that slayed not only your prince but many others in these last days. My daughter, your princess, has rid both kingdoms of her peril. Let us rejoice! From here out, both kingdoms shall unite lest another such trying to rob us of our happiness. Don't fret; you are not without royalty to guide you. My daughter shall rule this land, for she knows both worlds."

Turning to me, he smiles. "Ariel, I gift you both fin and feet to rule as you see fit between the two," he takes the blue stone from my hand, weaves a crown from water, and places it upon my head. "Rule with your heart, and you will never go wrong."

Wendell, Oli, and Storm step up to my sides. The King looks over them with a slight chuckle. "I'll need a sword to knight these companions of yours. Shall we name them your consorts?"

"Aye," I laugh. "That they are."

The crowd yells in excitement as Wendell helps

SINGING DAGGER

Eric's royal advisor aboard the Jolly. He then hands my father the sword Eric once carried at his waist.

I watch with a smile as each man is knighted, and they all arise with a smirk on their lips. The crowd cheers and claps once more.

I turn to my father, "Thank you, Daddy. I'm grateful for all your help and for never giving up on me."

My words bring a little tear to his eye, "You're my daughter on land or in the sea. Nothing will change that."

He raises a little higher on his wave so I can hug him, and he whispers in my ear. "I love you, Ariel, and I'm always proud of you."

"I love you, too, Daddy," I say as I release him. I watch as he disappears into the sea before turning my attention to my men and the crowds.

"Thank you all for the love and support. I will do my best to be fair, and just as we all adjust to life without my dearly departed Eric. This kingdom will never forget him, but now those who did this to him have met their justice, and as a people, we can heal together," I inform the crowd, to which I get more cheers. "Once life gets a bit more settled, I will be throwing a celebration to remember Eric, and you all are invited."

"That's nice of you, Lass," Wendell says as he moves closer to me.

"Eric may be gone, but his legacy will live on," I tell him honestly.

"As he shouldn't be," he agrees.

"Queen Ariel needs to get re-settled at the castle.

Let's disburse for now," the royal advisor tells the crowd, to which they boo a little.

"Thank you all for coming out," I call as they head back toward town and their home.

"Are you ready, my Queen?" the advisor asks.

"I am, but these three are coming with me. My consorts are to have access to everything in the castle just as I do," I inform him.

"Of course," he says with a little bow. "Once we are back in the castle, I will inform the rest of the staff."

"Thank you, and after you complete that, I'd like you to take the rest of the day for yourself," I tell him.

His eyes grow wide with fear.

"Do not fret. You aren't let go. I wish to ensure that all the staff has equal time off for rest and their families. I know what it's like go, go, go, and I don't want you or anyone in my charge running ragged," I state with a smile.

"That is a wonderful idea, my Queen," he says as he ushers me off the boat.

"You three are joining me, right?" I ask before making a move to leave the ship.

"If that is your wish, I will follow you," Storm says sweetly.

Wendell and Oli agree with an "aye."

"Then let's be off."

A few months later

"Ari-el, stop stressing," Sebastian states with a groan. "The castle and grounds are perfect for the celebration of Eric."

"Are you sure? When I walked by the courtyard, I didn't think there were enough flowers. What about the food? Are we going to have enough for all the people of Tirulia?" I question how many people live here.

"The chef is making extras as we speak. The castle is clean from top to bottom. You need to get dressed and get ready. Your consorts have been checking over all the details as well. If you keep it up, the staff will riot, and where would you be?" Sebastian says.

I let out a huff, and I know he is right. "Okay, you win. I'm heading to my chambers to get changed and ready. This is just the first big party I have put together, and it's for Eric and his memory. How can I live up to his shadow?" I ask honestly.

"Simple, you can't," Sebastian says bluntly. "You are not Eric, and I have seen all the time and planning you put into this. You, Ari-el, have honored his memory. Now it's time to leave his shadow and enjoy the sun on your face."

"Are you always right?" I laugh at my little crab friend.

"I'd like to think so," he smiles at me. "Now off with ya, time is ticking, and guests will be here soon."

"Yes, Sir," I joke as I make my way from the throne room towards my quarters.

It's taken me some time to adjust to ruling on land and having three men that love me at my side, but I'm doing it one day at a time. I long for a nice long swim in the sea; time just hasn't allowed that. My father has visited a few times, so I'm less seasick after seeing him. As much as I love my life, there's still an itch to return to the sea.

THE END

Thank you for reading our story. Check out the other stories in the shared world of Blades of Vengeance!

ABOUT THE AUTHORS:

ROWAN THALIA

My pen name is Rowan Thalia. I published my first novel on February 14, 2019.

I discovered very early on that I loved writing. Poetry was my first love and form of expression. I've written poems since I was sixteen and have quite the collection by now! Some of them you can find in my two poetry anthologies.

I've always been an avid reader and writer of short stories. My favorite author of all time is Anne Rice. In fact my pen name stems from one of her characters, Rowan, from The Witching Hour.

It wasn't until 2017, that I decided to push through and write a full-length novel. I started Binding Rayne (which went through several title changes at first) but struggled with the direction. In the middle of the first draft, I happened upon the reverse-harem book community on facebook. The complicated romances rooted in my author heart and before long, my book took on a new direction. The Keepers of the Talisman trilogy was born!

Since then, I have written and published many more reverse-harem romance novels, most of them paranormal in genre. Never to be one to sit idle, I've recently opened a second pen name—R. Thalia. With this name, I began the journey of writing my first (non-romance) paranormal thriller. I can't wait to break out and show the book world my full range of capabilities.

Thank you for all of the support and love that has been shown toward my book babies so far, I hope to keep surprising you with bigger and better projects!

Rowan's author page on amazon:
   http://author.to/rowanthalia

And her website:
   www.rowanthalia.com

JENÉE ROBINSON

Jenée Robinson has been married for over 20 years now, has three ornery girls, and lives on a cattle farm.
   Writing has always been one of her loves and she's excited to see where it takes her.
   She has completed several books, short stories, and has more releasing soon. She is busy writing more, so keep an eye out.

Other than writing, she loves reading and photography.

She's a Harry Potter Nerd and loves the show Supernatural and Captain America.

Jenée's author page on amazon:
https://www.amazon.com/Jenee-Robinson/e/B07BNC33ZB

Made in the USA
Columbia, SC
07 November 2022